book
tales

ALSO BY DAVID G. HALLMAN

Caring for Creation

AIDS—Confronting the Challenge

*A Place in Creation—Ecological Visions in
Science, Religion, and Economics*

Ecotheology—Voices from South and North

Spiritual Values for Earth Community

*August Farewell—The Last Sixteen Days
of a Thirty-Three-Year Romance*

Searching for Gilead—A Novel

book tales

SHORT STORIES BY
David G. Hallman

BOOK TALES
SHORT STORIES

iUniverse books may be ordered through booksellers or by contacting:

iUniverse
1663 Liberty Drive
Bloomington, IN 47403
www.iuniverse.com
1-800-Authors (1-800-288-4677)

ISBN: 978-1-5320-0248-9 (sc)
ISBN: 978-1-5320-0249-6 (e)

Library of Congress Control Number: 2016914131

Print information available on the last page.

iUniverse rev. date: 9/28/2016

A book is a dream that you hold in your hand.
— *Neil Gaiman*

Reading is the sole means by which we slip,
involuntarily, often helplessly, into another's
skin, another's voice, another's soul.
— *Joyce Carol Oates*

A writer only begins a book. A reader finishes it.
— *Samuel Johnson*

CONTENTS

PREFACE

I love to read books. I love to write books. So I decided to write a book about reading books.

I suppose that I'm self-centred as a writer. I'm more focused on my own desires when writing than I am on the reader's. I decided to craft a series of stories that would be fun to write, that would give me the opportunity to learn things about the books and their authors that I didn't know before, and that would force me to grapple with complex issues.

I wasn't wedded to making the stories consistently of the same genre. Some of the stories are fiction, some are creative nonfiction, and some are semifictionalized autobiography.

The process of writing the stories in *Book Tales* entertained and challenged me.

Hopefully you will be entertained and challenged when reading them.

David G. Hallman
Toronto, Canada

ACKNOWLEDGMENTS

I am indebted to the authors whose books inspired my writing of the stories in *Book Tales*.

I am grateful to people who read early drafts and provided helpful feedback, as well as to many others whose support and encouragement of my writing over the years has meant a great deal to me, including Elías Crisóstomo Abramides, Norman Abramson, Bill Aitchison, Gregory G. Allen, David Ambrose, Maureen Argon, John Philip Asling, Chuck Baker, Thean Beckerling, Brad Beckman, Stephen J. Belcourt, Ari Bendersky, Ed Bennett, Hammond Bentall, Daniel Benson, Janet Berkman, Murray Billet, Lorne Bobkin, David Bondy, Walter Borden, Michael Bourgeois, Enrique Alejandro Brieba, Linda Broadbelt, Sarah Bullick, Joan Burton, Ed Cabell, Grant Campbell, Alan Carr, Brenda Carr, Blaine Chaisson, Francis Chalifour, Richard Chambers, Joel Chapman, Tara Chapman, Richard C. Choe, Mark Citro, Mike Cobb, Bill Conklin, Marion Conklin-Griffith, Ray Coghlin, Shane R. Connor, Lichen Craig, Grant Cummings, Gail Czukar, Scott Dagostino, Joe Davies, Marie Day, Matt Dean, Frank Demois, Mary-Rose Donnelly, Nafisa D'Souza, Judy Dunn, Harold Durnford, Kergan Edwards-Stout, Winslow Eliot, Anne Elliott, Marg Erskin, Iben Evans, Ruth Evans, John Fagundes, Charles Fensham, Olga Fershaloff, Marco Fiola, John Flannery, Steven Forgacs, Roy Forrester,

John William Foster, Tim French, Michael Frieri, Armand Gagne, Damien Gajraj, David Garcia, Judi Gedye, Susan Gerhard, Tamara Glazier-Pariselli, Herb Gloutney, Aruna Gnanadason, Keith Goetsch, Donna Goldman, José Manuel de Juan González, John Goodhew, Fred Graham, Julie Graham, Joan Grant, Henrik Grape, Terry Greene, Diane Hallman, Jaye Hallman, Jim Hallman, Rick Hallman, Craig Hanna, Nancy Hardy, Mary Lou Harley, Bruce Harrigan, Drew Harris, Eldon Hay, Ron Hay, Michele Neff Hernandez, Jim Hodgson, Karin Hoeffken, Marilyn Hollinger, Judith Horner, Brendan Howley, Dorothea Hudec, Myke Hutchings, Moira Hutchinson, Roger Hutchinson, Glenys Huws, Carlos Idibouo, Jennifer Janzen-Ball, Christian Jasserand, Terry Jones, J. D. Kamran, Rahim Kanji, Dixie Kee, Guillermo Kerber-Mas, Joaquin Kuhn, Amos Lassen, Murray Laufer, Vanessa Laufer, Mary Leask, Marilyn Legge, Jason Lehmann, Michelle Lehmann, Gail Lerner, Jay Lesiger, David Levangie, Tilman Lewis, Christopher Lind, Emma Ruth Lind, Kristopher M. Lopez, David Lord, Murray Lowe, Joseph Luk, Jeffrey Luscombe, David MacDonald, Lee MacDougall, Bill MacKinnon, Allan Mailloux, Deborah Marshall, Jim Marshall, Wendell Martin, Ray McGinnis, Chris McIntosh, Barb McMahon, Joe McNally, Noel Mickelson, John Miller, Sebou Mirzayan, Alanna Mitchell, Danny Mitonides, John Montague, Kevin Morrow, Jesse Mugambi, Lynn Nagel, Maymar Naiman, Niki Nephin, Sarah Neville, Murray Newman, Lynda Newmarch, Rob Oliphant, Doug O'Neill, Kristján Hans Óskarsson, Alina Oswald, Harry Oussoren, Carol Paasche, Gottfried Paasche, James Patterson, Jeff Payne, Melissa Jo Peltier, Lillian Perigoe, Walter Pitman, Laura Pogson, Rafael Polinario, John Randall, Teresa Randall, Larry Rasmussen, Alan Ray, Chick Reid, Harald Roald, David Robertson, Ben Robinson, Martin Robra, Ashlyn Rodrigues, Alan Rodriguez, Dave Roger, Shauna Rolston, Stuart Ross, Jeffrey Round, John Russell, Bobby Sabitini, Stephen Scharper, Jeff Schmidt, Will Schwalbe, George Shafer,

Jake Sheepers, Vicky Sheepers, Susan Sheffield, Brandon Shire, John Shooter, Andy Sinclair, Deborah Sinclair, Donna Sinclair, Jim Sinclair, Chris Smid, David Snelgrove, Kamal al-Solaylee, Bronwyn Somerville, Darrel Sparkes, Hilaire St. Pierre, Yvonne Stewart, Harvey Swedlove, Simon Sykes-Wright, Erdal Tasuzan, Robert Thomson, Catherine Tillmann, Peter Timmerman, Doug Tindal, Mardi Tindal, Jack Urquhart, Kim Uyede-Kai, Dikky van der Ven, Claude Vidal, Melanie Votaw, Kim Westlake-Life, Allan Wilbee, Bev Williams, David Wilson, Lois Wilson, Susan Wiseman, Stephen Woodjets, Arthur Wooten, Ralph Carl Wushke, Joan Wyatt, Peter Wyatt, Marion York, Barbara Young, Denny Young, Ian Young, and Daniel Zaborski.

I appreciate the expertise and efficiency of the iUniverse staff who guided the production and publication of *Book Tales*.

tangier tryst

"WHY DON'T YOU STEP BACK FURTHER SO YOU can get Gibraltar in the picture?" Alistair cupped his hands to approximate the width of a rugby ball over his left shoulder. "Like about here."

"Why don't you take a flying leap over the railing?" Simon mumbled. He snapped the shutter without having stepped back and tossed the camera toward Alistair. Alistair lurched to his right, awkwardly trapping the camera against his body.

"Jesus, Simon, it could have gone overboard."

Simon walked back to the bench, out of the wind, and ran his fingers through his hair. Sitting down, he wrapped his scarf more tightly around his neck and pulled from his jacket pocket the dog-eared copy of *The Sheltering Sky* that he had picked up in a bookstall at the ferry terminal. He'd never read it and figured this was as good a time as any. He flipped it open to where his ticket stub was acting as a bookmark.

Alistair retrieved the camera case from where Simon had dropped it and slid the camera inside. He turned around, rested his palms on the banister, and watched the Rock diminishing in size as the ferry moved further from the Spanish coast. Shards of midafternoon sunlight slipped through the clouds and flashed onto the rock face. The slightest of drizzles, a fine mist, swept down from the sky and up from the sea. Alistair's glasses became speckled with moisture. He took them off, gripping them tightly in his gloved hand, closed his eyes, and tilted his head up into the wind. The cold and wet irritated his bald scalp. He winced but didn't move. *It's bracing,* he told himself.

He had made the crossing many times. Tangier had proven irresistible ever since his first exposure as a student 30-odd years ago—the chaotic vibrancy of the city, the exotic texture of the food, the clandestine sex with young Moroccan men on the beach and in the hills. And once his public school mate Rupert was appointed cultural attaché at the consulate, Tangier became a second home. They adored the city and each other. Never in bed though. Oh God, no, never with Rupert. Alistair shuddered at the thought.

This trip was different. He was no longer alone. For the first time, he would be in Tangier with a lover. He glanced over his shoulder to admire Simon on the bench, feeling this past year's intimate companionship suffuse his every pore, Simon's moodiness notwithstanding. Then immediately the pain of loss collapsed on top of him. Lady Priscilla, his mother, wasn't supposed to have died. Ever. She had been a force of nature all his life. For the first time, he wouldn't be sending a postcard home to her, jabbering to her on the phone about excursions into the desert, or anticipating an evening of cocktails and conversation at the manor on his return. Alistair smudged the vapour off his glasses and put them back on. He looked at Gibraltar, a metaphor for the state of his heart—monumental with his new love, scarred and crumbling with the loss of his mother.

He joined Simon on the bench and sat close enough so that their bodies were pressed lightly together. Simon didn't shift away. Alistair lifted his arm and wrapped it behind Simon's neck, resting it on top of the bench. He moved his hand down onto Simon's shoulder and gave it a squeeze. Simon slipped his ticket stub into his book and closed it. He raised his head, looked out at the sea, turned toward Alistair, smiled, and shrugged. Apology enough for Alistair. He smiled back.

The two of them had the upper deck pretty much to themselves. All the Moroccans were inside, protected from the blustery January winds; the scenery held no interest for them. Only a few other Westerners were on board. Suddenly, now in January 1991, North Africa had become a destination to avoid, what with the Gulf War in full swing.

If Simon had had his way, they wouldn't be here either, but not because of the war. Both Simon and Alistair considered the Westerners fleeing the region to be wimps. Rather, Simon had wanted to spend their break in Florence. He needed more time in the Uffizi library for his graduate thesis research on early Renaissance art. So he was in one of his moods.

Alistair needed to come to Tangier, and he was paying for the trip. While he was sorting through his mother's papers, he had come across a property deed from Tangier in her name— her maiden name—dated 1948, three years before he was born. She never mentioned having been to Morocco, a conspicuous and disquieting omission given Alistair's ravings about the country's allure.

For the past year since Simon and Alistair had become a couple, the latter usually acquiesced to the former's wishes. The mystery of the property deed meant that this time was an exception.

———

A mob of taxi drivers vying for business descended on them as they emerged from the ferry terminal. Alistair tried to use his limited Arabic, speaking well enough but not understanding the shouted responses.

After a few minutes, Simon turned to a driver who was grabbing at his luggage and asked, "Connaissez-vous Hotel el Muniria?"

"Mais oui, monsieur," the driver replied.

Simon released his bag into the driver's care, shouted at Alistair, "Come on, Alistair. Over here," and walked with the driver to his car at the curb. Alistair followed.

The driver took a circuitous route. Alistair frowned and clicked his teeth. Simon turned and looked out the window at the cacophony on the streets—the jostling of horse-drawn carts, dilapidated cars, dirty exhaust-spewing trucks and buses, bicycles and motor scooters weaving in and around the vehicles, women pedestrians wearing burqas, old men in djellabas, and groups of young men in jeans and track suits pushing and laughing, swigging on bottles and passing them back and forth, feigning boxing punches, their arms draped around each other's shoulders as they whistled at the occasional Western woman who would pass.

The taxi finally arrived at the small hotel's front entrance on the narrow rue Magellan. The driver fiddled for a few moments with the parking brake to ensure it engaged. Simon offered his arm to help steady Alistair as he struggled to get his footing on the street's steep incline. The driver yelled in Arabic toward the hotel entrance, and within a few moments a stocky young porter appeared. Alistair's hand, still resting on Simon's arm, twitched as they both watched Makmoud descend the few steps. "Bienvenue à l'Hotel el Muniria." Simon reached out his hand and shook Makmoud's. Alistair slipped his hand off Simon's arm, rested it on the car for support, and nodded. Makmoud smiled at them both and headed toward the boot to get the luggage.

The receptionist flushed as he examined Alistair's diplomatic passport. He said in heavily accented English, "Oh, Mr. Paddington. I'm so pleased you chose our humble hotel." Alistair grunted, signed the register, and headed toward the stairs leading up to their first-floor room. Makmoud waited for Simon, but Simon stepped aside, insisting that Makmoud go ahead. Simon then followed close behind, his gaze fixed on Makmoud's tight buns.

As Makmoud brought the luggage into their room, he rattled off the tourist spiel about William Burroughs and Allen Ginsberg having stayed at El Muniria. Alistair collapsed onto the bed, shut his eyes, and paid no attention. Almost immediately, he started to snore. After placing the bags on the luggage racks under the window, Makmoud tiptoed past the end of the bed and toward the door, where Simon stood holding out a 20-dirham tip. Makmoud titled his head in appreciation and reached for the bill. Simon didn't let go. A little tug-of-war ensued with the money.

"Est-ce que vous avez lu *Naked Lunch?*" Simon asked.

"Pardon?"

"William Burroughs's book, *Naked Lunch*. Have you read it? According to those photos in the lobby, he wrote it here at El Muniria." Both their hands still gripped the money, moving it back and forth between them in sync with the conversation.

Makmoud dropped his eyes. "Non, monsieur, je ne comprends pas l'anglais."

"Ah." Simon gave the dirham note an abrupt tug, which brought Makmoud stumbling closer. "Can I see you tonight? Sorry, I mean, est-ce que je peux te voir ce soir, peut-être?" Simon said quietly.

Makmoud stared at him hard for a moment. He looked over to the bed. Simon raised his fingers to his lips. "Shh. Je parle de moi seulement. Pas de nous deux." There was no way he was going to share hot, young Makmoud with Alistair—not that Alistair would permit a threesome in any case. Simon released his end of the note.

"D'accord, Monsieur Simon." Makmoud leaned in toward Simon, who, for a second, thought that he was about to be kissed. "Tu voudrais du kif, aussi?"

"Kif?"

Makmoud pinched his thumb and index finger together, raised the digits to his lips, and mimed a toke.

"Ah, oui. Très bien."

"Au toit, à minuit."

"Midnight is fine, but I'm sorry, where?"

Makmoud grabbed hold of Simon's arm and drew him out into the hallway, turning him to face a closed door at the far end of the frayed carpet runner. "L'escalier va au toit," he said, pointing his finger horizontally and then thrusting it upward at a 45-degree angle toward the roof terrace. Makmoud turned and, without another word, walked to the central staircase and back down to the lobby.

Simon stripped and headed into the bathroom to enjoy a shower after the hectic trip. He stood directly under the showerhead, letting the tepid water drizzle down his head, chest, and back. A croaking sound rumbled up through the pipes. He read the signal and stepped to the side as scalding high-pressure water cascaded out of the faucet, steaming the shower stall. Just like at home—the plumbing in their London flat operated precisely the same. He reached around the hot gushing stream and fiddled with the levers to get a more comfortable temperature, and then he stepped back underneath. With the more intense flow, water splashed beyond the shower curtain, wetting the bathroom floor. Alistair would be pissed. Also just like at home.

Simon stretched his head back in the shower, relishing the full force of the warmth on his face, and thought of Makmoud. He looked down and watched the water bouncing off his erection.

Flecks of croissant pastry dotted both their plates. Along the edges, smudges of butter and jam carried the indentation of small breakfast knives. Pulp from freshly squeezed orange juice clung to the ridges of two cloudy glasses that sat in the middle of the small round table. As he fingered the handle of his coffee cup, Alistair studied the faded and stained kilim-patterned cloth covering the table. He tried to determine whether the musty smell in the room was from the tablecloth or the dark turquoise velour curtains hanging behind him.

Simon raised his cup, paused, and with his left hand manipulated a page turn of *The Sheltering Sky*, which he had propped up against the edge of the table. He brought the coffee cup to his lips, took a sip, and set it down without interrupting his reading.

"Did you have a good run this morning?" Alistair asked.

"Uh-huh."

"Where did you go?"

Simon lifted his head out of the book. "What do you mean?" he asked. Alistair blinked, surprised at the sharpness in his voice.

"On your run. Where did you go?"

Simon returned to the book, read another few sentences, and turned the page. "The beach. Ran down to and along the waterfront."

"Ah." Alistair never objected to Simon's morning runs—he loved Simon's calves and thighs and buttocks—though there were pleasanter ways he'd like to begin a day than looking over at an empty side of their bed. On occasion back in London, Alistair had attempted to accompany Simon on a run, but his knees objected.

"How about if we get our coffee freshened and take it up onto the terrace?" Alistair suggested. The sombreness of the windowless bar that also served as the breakfast room had been a dismal environment in which to begin the day. "It'll be chilly, but at least we'll have a view across the rooftops to the sea."

"Hmm."

Alistair looked toward the beaded curtain hanging over the entrance to the kitchen and cleared his throat. He called, "Makmoud?" He waited. They were the only guests in the breakfast room. *No excuse for the service being so inattentive this morning*, Alistair complained to himself. He pushed back his chair and crossed over the room to the end of the bar. "Makmoud," he yelled.

Simon jerked his head up and pivoted around toward the bar. "For God's sake, what are you doing, Alistair?"

"Trying to get Makmoud's attention so we can have another cup of coffee."

"Oh." Simon turned back and buried his head again in the book.

The beaded curtain rattled and Makmoud appeared. "Oui, monsieur?"

"Makmoud. Deux cafés. Sur la terrasse, s'il vous-plaît."

"La terrasse?" Makmoud turned and, speaking in Simon's direction, added, "Sur le toit?"

"Oui, merci." Alistair headed toward the door. "I'm going to the room to pick up my jacket on the way up, Simon. Do you want me to grab yours?"

"Yes, please. I'll meet you up there." Simon stood, drained his cup, and then walked out of the room. Makmoud watched him as he passed.

Simon waited until Alistair reached the first floor and had turned the corner toward their room. He then bounded noiselessly up the stairs, taking two at a time, and rushed to the door at the end of the hallway. Once on the roof terrace, he looked around to get his orientation. He recognized the corner with the antenna and the pile of abandoned broken furniture. He hurried over and picked up the discarded tissues. Heading to the edge to toss them over, he hesitated and then turned back to examine the pebbled roof surface again. He found the used condom, dropped the tissues on top of it, and gathered the whole lot up. Checking over the wall, he tossed it all down onto the vacant rooftop of the building next door.

Moving quickly to the north side of the terrace, Simon arranged two of the chairs to face out toward the sea and placed a small table between them. He sat down and stretched his legs out in front of him. Standing up again, he dragged the chair a few inches closer to the edge so he could rest his feet on one of the low sections of the serrated wall. He opened the book and continued his reading.

Alistair arrived on the rooftop and paused to catch his breath. He approached Simon from behind and dropped Simon's jacket around his shoulders. Simon jumped. "Sorry, didn't mean to startle you, my dear," Alistair said. He rested his hands for a moment on Simon's shoulders and then leaned over and kissed the top of his head. Alistair moved over to the other chair and sat down. "You're really getting into that."

"Uh-huh, I guess. Kind of slow in parts."

"Paul Bowles is still living in Tangier, you know. He must be in his 80s by now. When we see Rupert at the consulate today, we could ask him about arranging for us to meet Bowles if you'd like."

"Uh, no, that's okay." Simon looked up from the book. "What do you mean, 'when we see Rupert'? You're assuming that I'm coming along?"

"Oh, Simon, for God's sake …" Alistair broke off as the terrace door opened and Makmoud appeared, carrying a tray with the two coffees. They both stared out toward the sea while Makmoud placed the tray on the table between them. "Thank you, Makmoud," Alistair said.

"Avec plaisir, monsieur," Makmoud replied. He glanced at Simon, catching sight of the back of his head.

As soon as Simon heard the terrace door close, he said, "You know, I can't stand Rupert. He gives me the creeps, and he's always so damned condescending to me. And of course with your history with him …"

Alistair rested the cup and saucer on his lap and took a sip of coffee. The sun had just broken through the heavy cloud cover. He leaned back, turned his head in the sun's direction, closed his eyes, and thought of Tangier in the good old days. Rupert was such fun to be with. No drama. Well, lots of drama actually, but always of the ebullient variety—scandalizing but then winning over the affection of merchants as they explored the souks together, and the artists whom Rupert introduced him to and with whom they would spend hours drinking and eating and debating the latest in art movements and influences. They'd spent long leisurely days on the beach in the warmer weather admiring the handsome young men and the virile not-so-young men—and then his solitary exotic nights meeting up with contacts made during the day.

Now, everything had to factor in Simon.

Stop romanticizing the past, Alistair scolded himself. *You're glossing over how lonely you were.*

Without opening his eyes, Alistair said, "Listen, Darling, I know you weren't keen to come here … but this is important … and I'd really appreciate your support."

"What, with your little archaeological expedition?" Simon dangled his arm down along the side of the chair, reached over, snapped his finger on the rim of his coffee cup on the small table, and watched the tiny wave vibrations. He snapped it again and then again, each time creating a pinging sound. Simon looked over at Alistair to see if that vein in his neck was twitching. It was. Ping. Ping.

"You still have your parents, Simon," Alistair said quietly. "Please, try to understand. This is … a bit difficult for me."

Simon gave the cup one last tap. He picked it up, took a sip, and then placed it back on the saucer. He shifted his chair to face the sun more directly and leaned back in a posture similar to Alistair's. "Yeah, I get that," he said. "But you don't really expect to find anything, do you? After all these years?"

Alistair sat up in his chair and looked at Simon. "Well, that's where Rupert comes in."

Alistair watched the muscles around Simon's mouth tauten. He knew how to get them to relax, but he also knew that Simon would not take well to an amorous advance at the moment, especially up here on the terrace. He found it surprising that the younger generation, or at least this particular example, seemed more sexually conservative than his own.

"I didn't mention it before we left London, but Rupert has been doing some sleuthing—he's got a lot of contacts from having been at the consulate here for so many years—and he says he has some leads about Mother's property."

Simon opened his eyes. "And …?"

"I'm skeptical there's anything to it, but I have to check it out. Mother never breathed a word about any property or even about having been here." *Damn it, why didn't you, Mother? We could have had such grand gabfests. And wouldn't it have been splendid to travel here together?* Alistair took off his glasses and poked his finger around his eye as if chasing a fleck of dust blown in by the breeze.

"And your father never spoke of it?"

"The deed is dated 1948 and they married in 1950. If she had some secret … from before they met … well, Mother was always so taciturn about personal matters. And then after Father was killed with Mountbatten in Ireland, she shut down further, refusing to talk about their history … or hers."

They sat in silence. Simon sipped his coffee and studied the sky. A fresh bank of clouds moving in from the Atlantic threatened to cover the sun soon. Simon got up and moved behind Alistair's chair, laid his hands on his shoulders, leaned over, and kissed the top of his head. "We should get going then. We're losing the sun anyway."

———

Rupert Carmichael, hands clasping his jacket lapels, stood at the top of the elegant marble staircase that rose from the street-level lobby of the British Consulate up to the first-floor suite of offices. Starkly bald except for tufts of white hair protruding out from behind his ears, he measured barely five foot five. The two lower buttons on his shirt were missing, exposing a clump of straggly hair around his navel. The head and lower-chest hair would have appeared iridescently white had his skin tone not been so pallid. As it was, the hair colour acted only as a punctuation mark against the sallow complexion. Everything about him was English white, except his teeth.

Simon giggled as they ascended the stairs, Rupert's cartoonish figure exaggerated all the more by their perspective of approaching him from below. Alistair, a step ahead of him, shot Simon a reprimanding glance over his shoulder.

"Alistair. Simon. You naughty, naughty boys." Rupert waddled down the top few stairs, his right hand clinging to the banister. "It's absolutely inexcusable that you didn't agree to stay with me." He reached Alistair and threw his arms around him, coming close to knocking both of them off balance. Simon leaned into Alistair's back, providing him extra support. Rupert stretched around each side of Alistair and grabbed hold of Simon's upper arms. "Yum. Someone's been working out." Simon shuddered but couldn't step away, being the stabilizer in the precariously balanced ménage à trois.

"Cut it out, Rupert," Alistair demanded with a feigned firmness. It was so good to see him. Alistair took the initiative to disentangle them all. He then led Rupert back up the stairs, grasping him securely by the arm. "This is Simon's first time in Tangier. I thought it better if he experienced the city by staying in a local hotel. We're at El Muniria."

"Oh, mon Dieu." Rupert scowled at Alistair as they walked arm in arm down the corridor. "You could have done much better than El Muniria." He looked back at Simon and winked. "My place, for instance, would have been so very much more comfortable than that flea-bitten hole."

Simon smiled at Rupert. "No problem. I'm appreciating the local colour of El Muniria."

Rupert furrowed his brow. Simon looked away.

"Please, have a seat," Rupert said as he ushered them into his office and headed behind the desk to answer the ringing phone on the credenza. He picked up the receiver, pressed the flashing button, listened for a moment, and then launched into an animated conversation that alternated between English and Arabic. Holding the phone in one hand, he gestured dramatically with his other as he talked and looked out onto rue Amerique du Sud below. Suddenly, he pulled the phone away from his ear and buried the receiver against his chest. He yelled out the open window, "Saqib, Saqib," and waved furiously at a young man in jeans, a white T-shirt, and a leather jacket who was heading into Café Dean directly across the street. The man looked up, squinted into the sun, and waved back.

Alistair and Simon examined the limited seating options. Two dark wooden chairs faced the desk, detailed fretwork running along their sides, the backs crowned by an elaborately carved oriental design. Worn mosaic-patterned cushions were barely visible on the seats, the edges peeking out from beneath haphazard piles of manila file folders, loose documents, dog-eared magazines, and yellowing newspaper clippings—much the same type of material that cluttered Rupert's large desk, save a small cleared space directly in front of his chair. A six-foot-long sofa abutted the bookcase. Propped up on the seat and resting against the sofa's back were 20 or so canvases—oil paintings and watercolours. On the floor in front of the sofa and leaning against the seat were others, these mounted in frames ranging from ornate gesso to simple nondescript wood.

Simon moved over to the sofa, carefully flipping through the canvases, scrutinizing a few closely. He lifted one of the unframed oils. Almost a quarter of the canvas was covered with a soft ochre sweeping diagonally across the upper left corner, a black vertical line severing it in two representing juxtaposed walls of an interior room. A rustic bed occupied most of the foreground, the headboard a dark wood butting up against the lighter walls. The bedcovering in pronounced green brush strokes gave few clues as to the fabric's texture or condition save the shadowing at the foot of the bed portraying the crumpled bottom portion and revealing a beige tick mattress beneath it. Sprawled across the bed was a pale naked figure, largely obscured impressionistically, but with sufficient detail to suggest gender and age—male and young.

Alistair watched Simon. He loved it that they shared a passion for art and that Simon knew so much about art history, more indeed than he did. It didn't bother Alistair much that there was no reciprocal interest from Simon in his work. Economics and the minutiae of trade negotiations were pretty boring stuff for most people. Not for Alastair, of course. He thrived in that world. But for someone like Simon, with that beautiful head of his in the clouds, Alastair's professional life was non-existent. No matter.

Rupert dropped the receiver back onto its cradle, turned, and plopped into his swivel chair. "This bloody war."

"What's happened?" Alistair asked as he approached the desk.

"Saddam's not only blowing up Kuwait's oilfields, but also he's about to sabotage my Tate Modern exhibition."

"What do you mean?" Alistair asked.

"Well, not Saddam. The mincing minions in the Foreign Office."

"That's rich," Simon mumbled under his breath.

Rupert looked up at Alistair and spat, "Your skittish colleagues at Whitehall don't think the time is right for an exhibit of Islamic artists from North Africa. What better time for culture exchange, I ask you, than when we're in a so-called clash of civilizations?"

"The war's not going to last long. Surely, they're overreacting."

"Well, you get right back to the office and convince them of that." Rupert swung his chair around and lifted up the receiver on the phone. "Can I book you a flight this evening?"

Alistair walked around the desk, took a hold of Rupert's hand,

and gently pried the phone out of his clenched fingers, putting it back on the cradle. He stood behind Rupert and began massaging his shoulders. "Goodness, old chap, you're tense."

Rupert closed his eyes. "Oh, that feels good. I miss your massages."

Alistair glanced toward Simon and shrugged.

"You know, Rupert, we on the trade side have nothing to do with the cultural department and their 'mincing minions.'" He lifted one hand and cuffed the back of Rupert's head.

"Ouch."

"Besides, I ..." Alistair looked over at Simon. "We ... have this personal business to deal with ... my mother's deed?"

Rupert sighed as he placed one hand on top of Alistair's hand that was still resting on his shoulder. Without opening his eyes, he turned his head and kissed Alistair's other hand. "Yes, I know, old boy. I'm sorry about Priscilla. She was always such a darling to me."

Simon placed the painting back on the couch and turned to leave.

Rupert raised his head up and looked at Alistair above him. "About the deed ..."

Simon stopped.

"Listen, Alistair," Rupert said, "I need a drink. Let's go over to Dean's and I can tell you what I've found out. Joe Dean's bar would be"—Rupert paused and stared up at Alistair—"an appropriate place to have this discussion, don't you think?"

"Huh?"

Rupert got up from his chair, sending Alistair stumbling back against the credenza. He turned and faced his friend. Grasping Alistair's elbows and pinning them to the side of his body, Rupert leaned in so his face was within inches of Alistair's. "To talk about Priscilla's deed at Joe Dean's ..." Alistair stared back blankly, his forehead furrowed.

Rupert shook his head and mumbled, "Geez."

"What?" Alistair asked. Rupert rolled his eyes and clicked his teeth. "Don't condescend to me," Alistair snarled.

Rupert dropped his arms, releasing Alistair, and moved around the end of the desk. "Let's go across the street," he said. "Besides, I want to introduce you to Saqib, my … ahem … gorgeous prodigy—gooorrrgeous—who's responsible for several of these pieces that you see on the sofa. He's basically self-taught, painting by instinct, as it were. I'd swear he's channelling Matisse's spirit." Simon was again holding the canvas he had picked up earlier, moving it within a few inches of his eyes and then further back. Turning toward Simon, Rupert said, "That's one of Saqib's. You know, my dear boy, Matisse spent time here in Tangier around 1912, 1913—thereabouts."

Without taking his eyes off the painting, Simon said, "Ah, yeah, Rupert, I'm aware of that."

Rupert slapped his hands against his cheeks. "Oh, Saqib will be fit to be tied if the Tate show gets cancelled."

He looped his arm through Alistair's, hauled him toward the door, and slipped his other arm around Simon's waist. Simon squirmed. Rupert smiled and tightened his grip. "Not a word about the Tate issue to Saqib."

Rupert suddenly stopped and scurried back to the desk. Picking up the receiver and pressing the intercom button, he waited a moment and then said, "Jocelyn. Rupert here. Could you try to get a message over to Paul Bowles? See if he's up to coming to the consulate for tea tomorrow." He paused. "Huh?" There was another pause while he listened. "Oh, say three o'clock. That means he'll maybe get here by four. That's a dear."

Beaming, he hung up the phone. "See, Alistair my dear," he said while looking at Simon, "I didn't forget."

Simon frowned at Alistair. Alistair smiled weakly at Simon and said, "I thought that you'd like that."

Rupert joined Alistair and Simon at the door, squeezing in between them, repositioning his one arm through Alistair's, and putting his other arm around Simon's waist. The three of them walked awkwardly in tandem toward the staircase. Rupert said, "How does that go in *The Sheltering Sky?*" He screwed up his mouth and tilted his head to the side as he tried to remember. "Port says to Kit something like … um … 'We're both afraid of life' … No, that's not quite right: 'We're both afraid … to get all the way into life.' That's it. That's it. 'We're hanging on to the outside for all we're worth, convinced we're going to fall off …'" Pressing his weight down on Alistair's arm and Simon's waist, Rupert boosted himself up and clicked his heels, almost sending the three of them careening down the stairs. "'Getting all the way into life.' I love that line."

———⌒———

As the trio stepped out of the consulate, dozens of exhaust-spewing scooters roared down the street, each with two or three young men perched atop, hollering and brandishing Moroccan flags and pendants of the IR Tangier football team. Alistair jumped backwards toward the consulate door. Rupert, squealing and laughing more loudly than even the roar of the bikes, pivoted around toward Simon and pinned him against the building wall. Simon thrust his arms across his face as debris flew and gritty fumes threatened to choke him. Rupert buried his head in Simon's chest.

The last of the bikes passed. Simon, trapped in Rupert's clutches, raised his arms and glared down at him. Rupert, ignoring the hostility, threw his head back and yelled, "God, I love this town." He stepped away from the wall and turned toward Alistair, who was still cowering near the consulate doorway. "When did you get so soft, old man?" With his eyes twinkling as he looked back and forth between Alistair and Simon, he added, "Is this what married life does to you?"

Alistair grumbled, "Harrumph," and strode purposefully

down the few steps to the street level, brusquely brushing the dust off his sports jacket.

Rupert opened his arms and embraced the street, his left welcoming the re-emerging pedestrian traffic, his right regretfully bidding adieu to the young men as the last of the dust settled and the sound of engines and shrieks faded. "This is life! By God, this is life. Get into it. All the way into it." He pirouetted and headed through the beaded curtain of Dean's entrance.

Alistair and Simon followed him and stood just inside the entrance, letting their eyes adjust to the darkness. The air was leaden, acrid tobacco smoke overlaid with a sweet hashish smell and a damp woolen mustiness. Blue and white tiles, chipped and stained, ran up the walls about four feet. Higher up hung old framed photographs featuring clusters of partygoers of years past.

A few scruffy young people leaned on the bar, their backpacks resting at their feet as they spoke to each other in Spanish. Local Moroccans sitting at the first few tables on the left side stopped talking to stare at Alistair and Simon.

Rupert was sitting with Saqib near the back. A couple of beers, a pot of tea, and four stained glasses were already on the table. He gestured to Alistair and Simon. "I presume you realize that you are on hallowed ground, my young friend," he said to Simon as he pushed out the chair next to him and patted the seat. "Sit, sit."

The sound of another chair scraping the floor caught Simon's attention. Across the table, a pair of eyes with irises so dark they were indistinguishable from the pupils had locked onto his. Short black bristled hair covered Saqib's head, arching across the forehead, slicing around the temples, and skirting down behind the ears. The rigidly straight-lined nose was disproportionately large, as were the full lips. With a slight twitch of his head, Saqib motioned toward the empty chair beside him. Simon mumbled, "What do you mean, 'hallowed ground'?" as he squeezed between the table and the adjacent one to get to the seat offered. Saqib's knee grazed against Simon's as he sat down.

Rupert looked down at the table, breathed in and out, and then said in a chipper fashion, "Alistair and Simon, let me introduce you to my very good friend Saqib."

Simon shook Saqib's hand. "I saw a few of your paintings in Rupert's office. Stunning."

"Thank you. I have more that I could show you." Saqib tightened his grip. Simon flinched and squeezed back, hard. Saqib did not flinch.

"Yes, I'd be interested to see more."

Alistair sucked his teeth and leaned over the table, his hand suspended above the others. "Glad to meet you, Saqib." Saqib let go of Simon's and shook Alistair's hand. Alistair sat down beside Rupert.

"In answer to your question, Simon, my boy, so many glitterati have graced these premises ..." Rupert paused and mockingly fluffed his hair. "So many came here to drink, cruise, and gossip long into the night. Errol Flynn, Ava Gardner, Francis Bacon, Cecil Beaton, Barbara Hutton, Paul Bowles and his protégé Ahmed Yacoubi ..." Rupert reached across the table and patted Saqib's arm. "Jane Bowles and Cherifa, her—what shall we say?—companion ... psycho temptress ... whatever. Truman Capote, Ian Fleming, Tennessee Williams, Jean Genet, Samuel Beckett, Allen Ginsberg, Jack Kerouac, William Burroughs. But Dean wouldn't serve Burroughs ... took an immediate dislike to him, disapproving of Burroughs's druggy habits." Rupert wagged his finger back and forth at Simon and Saqib. "Let that be a warning to you youngsters."

"Yes, yes," Simon interrupted. "I get the point. Hallowed ground. I apologize for not kissing the floor when I entered."

Rupert rolled his eyes and turned toward Alistair. "My, my. Is your boy toy always so testy?"

"Fuck you, Rupert," Simon growled.

"Tsk, tsk, Simon." Rupert chuckled, tilting his head in Alistair's direction. "You should have learned by now to be more respectful to your elders. Anyway, dear old Joe Dean knew all the best gossip in town and told outrageous stories to divert attention from his own nefarious carryings-on, which, rumour has it, ran the spectrum from being a gigolo and drug smuggler to first-class espionage."

Alistair noticed that Saqib had only one hand resting on the table. Simon took a swig of his beer while looking skeptically at Rupert. "Sounds a bit farfetched," he said, setting his beer back down and sliding it back and forth between his two hands before letting his right hand drop onto his lap.

"Apparently," Rupert continued, clapping his hands together lightly, "he'd listen in to the deals being made by some of the shady characters in his bar at night, and ships would mysteriously be blown up later in the harbour. There are all kinds of stories of him feeding information to various intelligence services before and during World War Two. It's said that Joe was the model for the bartender Rick in the movie *Casablanca*, the character played by Humphrey Bogart."

Alistair frowned at Rupert. "Okay, Rupert. Enough jabbering. Can we get down to business?"

"Well, I'm just paying tribute to Joe's spirit and the spirits of so many others," Rupert said, lifting his arms up toward the ceiling as if invoking these deities of old, "including Priscilla's."

"What about Mother?" The sharpness in Alistair's voice was followed immediately by a darkness sweeping across his line of vision. He blinked several times and it dissipated. He raised his hand nonchalantly to massage the twitching vein in his neck.

Rupert looked over one shoulder and then the other. He leaned forward and motioned to the others to come in closer.

"Rupert, for Christ's sake, cut the melodrama." Alistair slapped his hand against the edge of the table. Tea splashed out of the glasses. "Honestly, you can be such a buffoon at times."

Sitting back and turning toward Alistair, Rupert stared at him with stone-cold eyes and said nothing.

Chatter continued at other tables and at the bar. Protestations of a braying donkey and the cackling of crated chickens tethered to its back protruded in from the street. Saqib sipped his tea. Simon turned his head in his direction, ostensibly to look toward the door and the commotion in the street. Using his left hand, Simon lifted his beer for another swig, blocking in the process Alistair's view of his face. Alistair dropped his eyes and drummed his fingers on the table.

"Habibi," Saqib said, softly focusing on Rupert. "Habibi, tell them what you've discovered."

Alistair jerked his head toward Saqib. "You know?" He turned back toward Rupert.

Saqib reached across the table with both hands and gently palmed the back of Rupert's hand. "Habibi," he repeated more quietly than before. Rupert looked down at their clasped hands and then raised them up off the table. He planted a quiet kiss on the back of Saqib's hand.

Alistair stood up, his chair clattering to the floor behind him. "For Christ's sake, Rupert." Heads throughout the bar turned and looked.

Rupert stared up at Alistair as he gently placed Saqib's hand back down on the table.

"Okay. I have something to show you," he said quietly. "We'll grab a taxi."

Saqib said, "I've got my motorcycle. You can come with me, Simon."

"Sure," Simon replied and headed toward the door with Saqib.

"Be careful," Alistair called after them. "Do you have helmets?"

Rupert shook his head. "Jesus, Alistair, you are such an innocent." He turned and walked out into the street. Alistair hesitated for a moment and then followed after him.

Neither of them spoke as the taxi wound up the road into the lush hills of Old Mountain, each staring out his side of the car at the villas of wealthy Moroccans and foreigners. Stone walls, drenched in cascading vines, masked most of the sumptuous homes. Crumbling masonry allowed glimpses of a few neglected properties. Top-heavy palm trees punched the sky, interspersed with windswept Aleppo pines and obelisk cedars. Occasionally, the rich plant growth stuttered, affording Alistair a brief view of the Straits of Gibraltar out past the coastal bluffs.

"C'est bien, monsieur," Rupert said. "You can stop just behind those two gentlemen up ahead."

Alistair glanced over at Rupert and then out through the front windshield. Saqib was sitting on his motorcycle by the curb. Simon stood astride the front wheel, resting his hands on the handlebars. He was looking toward the sea, following Saqib's gestures through a narrow break between two properties. As the taxi pulled up, Simon moved back from the bike and straightened up. Saqib stayed seated. They both watched Alistair and Rupert get out of the car.

Rupert walked up to Saqib and rested his arm on his shoulder. Alistair cleared his throat. "So?"

Rupert grabbed Saqib's hand and steadied him as he dismounted the bike. They turned and started walking hand in hand along the narrow path. "Watch your step," Rupert called over his shoulder. Simon immediately followed. Alistair didn't move. His hands lodged in his trouser pockets, he stared after the three figures receding down the steeply inclined slope.

"Monsieur," the taxi driver called to Alistair. "Monsieur?"

Alistair turned and looked at the driver, who was leaning out the car window. "Oh yes, please wait."

He scurried after the others, carefully holding on to stunted trees and protruding boulders, slightly disoriented by the claustrophobic effect of the high walls on either side. Suddenly, the path broke out onto a clearing that extended expansively to the right and left, and two hundred or so metres straight ahead, before disappearing down an incline. The ground was barren save the occasional scrub brush jutting out of crevices in the stone. It appeared as the reverse of an oasis—a desiccated strip of land bordered on either side by the opulent growth that was visible behind well-tended walls of the neighbouring properties.

The others, standing near to where the plateau dropped off, were looking at the stunning, unobstructed view of the Straits of Gibraltar. Alistair stayed back, folding his arms across his chest and shuffling his feet to smooth the ground and secure his footing. A brisk wind was blowing in from the Atlantic.

Rupert turned around and called back to Alistair, "What do you think of your property?"

The wind had strengthened. Alistair cupped his hands behind his ears and hollered, "What?"

Rupert turned and walked back toward him. "This land belongs to you, Alistair, you lucky, undeserving bastard," he said. He stopped, hands on hips, about six feet from Alistair. "Courtesy of Lady Priscilla, the mother it seems you hardly knew, and her lover Joe Dean."

Alistair stared at Rupert, totally immobilized until he wasn't. As soon as Rupert saw the telltale movement of the eyeballs rolling back behind the lids, he rushed to catch Alistair just as he collapsed, shaking, onto the hard ground. With one arm wrapped around Alistair's back, Rupert manipulated his linen handkerchief out his pocket with his other hand, rolled it across Alistair's gyrating chest into a tubular mass, and slipped it between Alistair's teeth, the ends dangling out each side of his mouth and rapidly getting drenched in white phlegm.

Simon and Saqib, their conversation and their enjoyment of the vista interrupted by Rupert's cries for help, rushed to the pair and knelt on each side of Alistair's head, their four hands intertwining underneath and supporting his head.

The consulate lounge was deserted, as it had been for the past couple of weeks since the Gulf War began. There were no visiting dignitaries to host, no cultural receptions to sponsor. The heavy brocade drapes were drawn across the floor-to-ceiling windows, slivers of late afternoon sunlight trespassing into the room where the worn fabric had pulled loose of the wooden hooks. In a far corner, half a dozen chairs circled a large hexagonal coffee table. The burnished walnut surface bore scars of more robust occasions, a few of which had discoloured the inlaid mother-of-pearl.

"I told Jocelyn not to have them serve the tea until we were all here." Rupert spoke quietly, his hand resting on Alistair's forearm. In the chair beside Rupert, Alistair sat slumped, staring at the design on the coffee table. "Munir, my friend from the land registry office, often runs late. When he shows up, Jocelyn will bring him and Teddy, our consular lawyer, in here together. Hopefully, Simon and Saqib will be here by then."

Alistair lifted his head and frowned at Rupert.

"I'm sure they'll come, Darling." Rupert patted Alistair's arm. Alistair moved his arms off the chair's armrests and dropped his hands into his lap. "I must say, though," Rupert continued, "I think it's bloody inconsiderate of Simon to have left you alone all last night after your ... seizure."

Alistair looked up at the ceiling, squinting through the low light at patches where the mosaic patterns had deteriorated exposing flaked and water-stained plaster. "Don't be too hard on him," Alistair said, studying the ceiling with the intense scrutiny of a conservation restorer. "He knows that I'm always dead to the world for hours after an episode. There's nothing he could have done for me if he had been home, I mean, at the hotel."

"All the same, he should have ... Well, I wish you had let me stay with you, if not for your comfort, at least for my peace of mind."

Alistair smiled at Rupert. "That's kind of you, my dear."

"When I last saw him and Saqib tearing off into the Medina

on the motorcycle, I just assumed they were using a shortcut to the hotel that we couldn't take in the taxi. Saqib knows that maze of tiny streets like the back of his hand."

Alistair closed his eyes, took in a deep breath, and held it.

Jocelyn's clearing her throat brought both their attention to the doorway. Through the opaque light of the cloistered room, Alistair could make out the silhouettes of several people highlighted against the brightness of the hallway outside. He smiled and let out his breath. *We'll get through this,* he thought. *Actually, this may be the start of a whole new chapter in our lives, unexpected to be sure, but an adventurous direction to be grasped with relish and vigour. It's a good omen that my energy is returning more rapidly than it usually does after an episode.* Alistair went to get up, felt dizzy, and sat back down again. *Don't rush it.*

"Ah, good, they're here," Rupert said as he stood up and began walking toward the door. "Come in, come in." The figures didn't move. "Ah, Paul, too," he exclaimed as he reached the group. He turned back and faced Alistair. "How reprehensible of us, Alistair. With all the excitement, we forgot that we had invited Bowles for tea today." Turning toward the door, he extended his hand and grasped Paul Bowles's hand. "Come in, come in. Please forgive our tawdry manners, Paul. We've had a bit of a hectic time over the past 24 hours." Bowles said nothing. Still holding his hand, Rupert craned his neck to identify the others standing so solemnly.

Edward Scott, the consular lawyer, stepped forward out of the shadows. "Rupert ..." he began, and then stopped. Jocelyn stifled a whimper.

"Yes, Teddy," Rupert enthused, "we'll get into the details in a moment. Let's all sit and have some tea first. Come in, come in, the rest of you."

Scott took a few steps into the room and looked uncertainly back and forth between Rupert and Alistair. Addressing Alistair, he nodded and said, "Mr. Padington ... sir ..."

Alistair smiled and nodded back.

"Mr. Padington … and Rupert … I'm sorry to have to inform you … there's been an accident."

———⌣———

Alistair lifted his legs slightly up off the chaise lounge, stretched them out, and pointed his toes toward the sea. He held them there for a few moments and then raised his knees up toward his chest, clasping his arms around his legs when he got them as close to his chest as possible. After the surgery in London, the physiotherapist had recommended this exercise as one of several to help him adjust to the new knees. He didn't like to visualize those metal joints swivelling around inside his legs, but he certainly liked the relief that they afforded. The osteoarthritis had become so severe that he was at risk of not being able to manoeuvre the steps from the road down to the new house.

Rupert's incessant haranguing had become almost as intolerable as Alistair's physical pain. "You spend a fortune building this villa," Rupert would say, waving his hand around at the chaos of construction materials covering the site, "but you won't afford yourself the luxury of spending a pittance on some reconstructive surgery so that you can enjoy it."

"Fifteen thousand pounds is hardly a pittance."

"Well, if you weren't such a classist and were willing to go to a public hospital, it wouldn't have cost you a farthing."

"A farthing?" Alistair hooted. "What century are you living in?" They glared at each other, testing to see who would blink first. They broke simultaneously and doubled over in laughter.

This argument or a variation thereof was reprised countless times from the day that they had first trampled around the Old Mountain lot with the architect. It had become patently clear that Alistair's deteriorating joints would give no end of trouble, even once the rocky path was replaced with smooth marble steps and the rough terrain of the property was covered in the house's gleaming terra cotta floor tiles.

Five years. He hadn't expected it would take that long. But now in the post-construction silence, with the only sound being the breeze through the neighbouring trees, he basked in the June warmth and looked out at the royal blue sea that grounded the jagged outline of the Spanish coast beyond and the azure blue sky above. It was so worth it. He unclasped his arms, stretched out his legs, and wiggled his toes.

My God, I'm actually twiddling my toes in delight. He giggled to himself.

The moment of un-nuanced pleasure flitted away, replaced not with the gut-wrenching grief that had predominated for so long but rather with the dull ache of a melancholy that was becoming his more consistent companion. Many people never in their lives feel the passionate love that he had for Simon. That's what he told himself, and so many others did as well, in the weeks and months—and now years—since the accident. As if that was supposed to console him. It hadn't. Rather, it had made him greedy for more.

Rupert was better at moving on. *Don't be so presumptuous,* Alistair scolded himself. Rupert was just less blatant in his grief at losing Saqib. He no doubt felt as intensely the cleaver that rent both their hearts the day Saqib's motorcycle had skidded under the wheels of that rumbling camion in the Medina. Saving Alistair from drowning in his mourning had been Rupert's priority, succeeded then by holding his hand during the long years of designing and building the villa. Alistair and his dramas had been quite the handful for Rupert.

A smile flickered across Alistair's face. Building the house for both of them to live in and thereby enticing Rupert out of his squalid apartment was Alistair's thank-you to his old friend. Maybe someday, he'd say a thank you out loud. Maybe not. Surely Rupert understood.

Neither of them had passionate young lovers anymore. But they had each other. It was a compensation, of sorts.

References

Bowles, Paul. *The Sheltering Sky.* New York: John Lehmann Co., 1949.

Dillon, Millicent. *You Are Not I—A Portrait of Paul Bowles.* Los Angeles: University of California Press, 1989.

Green, Michelle. *The Dream at the End of the World—Paul Bowles and the Literary Renegades in Tangier.* New York: Harper Collins, 1991.

strong like tessa

THE HEADLIGHT BEAMS SWEPT ACROSS THE bedroom ceiling as Trevor pulled up the inclined driveway. Cheryl, propped up in bed with two pillows behind her back, looked up from the page and watched as the brilliant shafts came to a standstill on the far wall, catching the corner of the dresser mirror and jarring the whole room into a halogen glare.

When only the nightstand lamp was on, little was visible beyond the bed. Cheryl treasured the cocoon of amber light drifting from over her right shoulder down onto the page and then spilling out for just a few feet of the burgundy comforter that covered her jackknifed knees.

The truck's arrival always changed that. The wall around the mirror exploded to life with the spotlighting of framed pictures of Trevor's triumphs—bronco ridings, moose hunts, prizewinning trout catches. Most of them were showing their age—the newspaper clippings yellowing, the colours in the grainy Instamatic photos dulled, the printed versions of old slides warping ever so slightly off the frames' backing. The razor-sharp white intensity of the truck's headlights exaggerated these testaments to time's passage. Of course Trevor never experienced this startling moment because he was always in the truck. Cheryl never didn't notice.

She also noticed, more frequently of late, the unfamiliarity of the Trevor beaming out from the photographs. The guy holding up the 23-pound rainbow trout or leaning against the massive antler head or suspended six inches above the saddle pumping his hat skyward was a stunning hunk of man—bristling black hair and moustache, mouth wide open in an ever-present laugh, broad shoulders and powerful chest punching through even the loosest of clothing. But it was mainly the riveting eyes full of sexual energy and exuberance that captured her. In every picture, he was looking directly into the camera as if declaring, "This one's for you, Cheryl, Baby."

Cheryl lifted the covers and looked down at her own body, what she could make out of it under her pyjamas. There were a few extra pounds around her midriff that had not been there when she first caught Trevor's eye six years ago. She slipped her hand under her pyjama top and pinched the skin at her waist. She let go and spread her palm wider to get a larger grip. Well, maybe more than a few extra pounds. So they both had changed. Life happens.

She turned down the corner of the page she was on, slowly closed the book, and did not move from the bed lest he see her shadow through the sheers.

The thumping base from his sound system acted like grounding for the idling motor. She knew that he would sit in the pickup for another few minutes finishing the beer he'd absconded with after receiving a wink from Joe the bartender—the one-for-the-road finale to his Friday night spent at the bar with his buddies.

The headlights went out, but the music and motor continued to rumble.

She waited.

Then she heard silence, followed seconds later by the creaking open and the slamming shut of the truck door.

Cheryl darted out of bed, crouching down as she passed the window to get to the safety of the closet on the far side of the room. She reached up and lifted the afghan on the shelf, ready to slip the book underneath. Hesitating, she focused on the picture on the cover, whispered "Strong like Tessa" to herself, and then slipped John le Carré's *The Constant Gardener* into its hiding place.

Sensing a slight pressure of having to pee, she cursed herself for not taking a break earlier from her reading. There was no time now. She scurried back to bed, slipped under the sheets, turned off the lamp on the nightstand, and pulled the comforter up to her neck. A moment later, the bedroom door swung open. Trevor strode in, burped, and said, "You still awake, CC? Get it hot, Baby. Get it hot."

Cheryl made muted snoring sounds as Trevor plied off his boots and kicked them into the corner. The reek of his work socks caught in her throat. She stopped breathing altogether to stifle a cough. Trevor grunted, struggling to pull his sweatshirt up over his head. He lost his balance momentarily and bumped into the dresser. "Shit."

His belt made a slight ting as he unbuckled it. Cheryl waited for the dreaded slithering sound of leather against denim, were he to yank the belt out of the pant loops. She relaxed when she heard only the opening of the zipper and the clunk of his pants once they slid down his legs and hit the floor.

The bed jiggled as Trevor collapsed onto it. He lay on his back, breathing loudly and rapidly, partly still chilled from the cold March air outside and partly recovering from the exertion of undressing. After a few moments, he rolled over to Cheryl's side, putting his arm around her and thrusting his pelvis up against her buttocks. She twitched involuntarily as his erection jabbed her, a blunt knife even through the comforter, the sheets, and her pyjamas. Warm beer breath swamped Cheryl's cheek. "Okay, Babe, Big T's ready." Placing his right hand on her head and running his fingers through her hair, he reached with his left across her body and yanked the comforter and sheet off her. "Jesus, you got those fuckin' flannels on."

Cheryl turned her head toward him and let out an exaggerated yawn. "Oh, you're home, Darling," she said without opening her eyes.

He gripped her hair tightly while his other hand made its

way under the elasticized waistband and into her panties. His fingers snaked around for a few moments before he jerked them out, snapping the waistband against her midriff. "Goddammit, you're dry as fuck. I'll get grease."

He rolled off her, huffed out of bed, and headed into the adjoining bathroom.

Please let him bring the K-Y, Cheryl prayed. She heard no drawer open. That meant he'd grabbed the scented hand lotion from on top of the counter. She'd have an irritation tomorrow.

———

Cheryl hadn't heard of *The Constant Gardener* before the Oscar Awards the previous weekend when Rachel Weisz won Best Supporting Actress.

At work the day after the Oscars, her friend Patty was still on an Oscar high, ecstatic that Reese Witherspoon had won Best Actress for playing June Cash in *Walk the Line.* "Fantastic, fuckin' fantastic. How often do they make a movie about us folks? I'd see it a hundred times if I could." Patty, with whom Cheryl shared so much—a desk at work, most lunch hours, and an abridged version of her personal life—had already seen *Walk the Line.* Twice. Cheryl hadn't—not *Walk the Line* or any other recent film.

"What do you mean, 'us folks'?" Cheryl laughed, shifting the in-tray a shade so that she could perch on the lip of Patty's side of the desk. "Johnny and June Cash were southerners. Bet they never set foot in Wyoming. It was that other film that took place here. What's-it *Mountain.*" She grimaced and gave her body a little shudder.

"I don't mean us Wyoming folk," Patty said. "I mean us country-and-western folk." Patty grabbed hold of Cheryl's arm and gave it shake. Cheryl looked at Patty's hands, admiring the work done by the manicurist in the strip mall beside their office— oversized fingernails, currently rocket red, long enough to emit a soft click on the computer keys when she typed. Cheryl shifted her hand to hide her own nails. Everything about Patty was oversized: bleached blond hair billowing down to several inches below her broad shoulders; luminescent green eyes accented by jet-black lashes and meticulously applied mascara; a set of the largest lips Cheryl had seen on anyone, attentively coloured daily to coordinate with her nails. Cheryl suspected collagen. And, of course, there was the double-D brassiere size.

Cheryl glanced around Cheyenne's Social Security Office to see if Mr. Slate's door was open. The boss's door was shut. In the outer office, a client was kicking up a ruckus, but the ever-patient Mabel was handling him. Ray, dapper as always in his pressed security uniform and crisp white shirt fraying slightly around the collar, stood discreetly off to the side, keeping a watchful eye. No one in the office knew how old Ray was except for Mr. Slate, who had fudged the regulations to allow him to keep working.

Cheryl turned back toward Patty and whispered, "Isn't it so yukky about that *Mountain* movie? Now the world thinks our Wyoming men are a bunch of faggy cowboys."

Patty rolled her eyes. "Oh, my dear, sweet, innocent child. Have you seen *Brokeback Mountain*? Oh, what am I saying—of course, you haven't. You wouldn't believe how hot it was watching those two dudes going at it. I got moist sitting in my seat. Heath Ledger is such a ... Grrr." Patty braced her hands on the desk, lifted her bum slightly off the chair, and thrust her pelvis forward in three powerful jerks. "And with cute-tight-buns Gyllenhaal. Yum. Yum." She dropped back into her chair, lifted a file folder, and fanned herself.

Cheryl's hand shot to her mouth as she giggled through her fingers. "Patty May Connor, don't be so gross." Patty wasn't paying attention. Her eyes were closed, her lips puckered in a tight grin, her body swaying back and forth.

"Cheryl to Patty. Come in please."

"Ahhhh." Patty opened her eyes and looked up at Cheryl, giving her one of those guileless smiles of which she had an inexhaustible supply. "Well, I can dream, can't I? A threesome with those two. I'd sell my soul." She sighed. "Do you suppose there are pictures of them going at it on the Internet? Oh yeah, the movie trailer that they showed last night."

Patty's fingers raced onto her keyboard. She Googled "Oscars."

Cheryl grabbed her chair and wheeled it over next to Patty so she could see her computer screen. "Ta-da," Patty said as she scrolled through the Oscars Web site.

Cheryl heard her but made no response. Her eyes had caught sight of a photo of Reese Witherspoon and Rachel Weisz side by side, grinning affectionately at each other, holding their respective Oscars. Like a preset montage, the video clips of Witherspoon in *Walk the Line* and Weisz in *The Constant Gardener* started reeling through her memory. Strong women. The mini-retrospective looped through a second time in her head and then resolved down, focusing only on *The Constant Gardener* film images of Weisz. She recalled Tessa laughing with her husband, British career diplomat Justin Quayle, played by Ralph Fiennes; Tessa soaking in a bathtub as he leaned over the edge, lovingly massaging her pregnant abdomen; Tessa walking through the Nairobi slums with her medical bag; Tessa arguing with authorities about collusion between the government and a pharmaceutical multinational to use poor Nigerians as guinea pigs in a risky drug trial; strains in their marriage, with Justin caught between his wife's activism and his professional obligations to his bosses; Tessa standing up to everyone, on principle, and it costing her marriage; and more.

Patty cupped Cheryl's chin and gently forced her head up from the computer screen to face her own. "Honey, are you okay?" she asked quietly.

"Huh? Oh. Oh yeah. Excuse me. I have to go to the toilet. Be right back."

On the way home that evening, Cheryl stopped by the library and checked out a copy of *The Constant Gardener*.

Cheryl turned her head and glanced at the clock on her nightstand, but it was still too dark to make out the time. She would have had to roll over, reach out, and press the illuminating button on the top. She didn't want to make such disruptive a movement. For all his bulk, Trevor was a light sleeper. Having him curse her out for waking him on a Saturday morning was not an appealing way to begin the day.

She lay quietly.

Her side of the bed rose and fell in sync with his breathing. A rasping intake of breath through his mouth, guttural and phlegm-sounding, coincided with a depressing of his two-thirds of the bed and a concomitant rise of a few inches on her allotted portion. His exhaling, marginally quieter, lasted longer and was accompanied by a gentle depositing of her back to the mattress's normal height. Cheryl found the repetitive movement and predictable sounds almost tranquil—far more pleasant than the angry snores of last night as he fell asleep after the sex, still drunk.

She was contemplating buying a bigger bed that would give her more room. This double-size mattress was the one that she and Rob had bought when they first rented the house before the wedding. Their friends who had helped them move the furniture in had great fun teasing Cheryl about the risks, now that they had a bed, of Rob seducing her before they were legally husband and wife. She never told anyone, nor did she think Rob ever did, that they in fact made love for the first time on the moving day after everyone else had left. The circumstances were so romantic and Rob had been so patient that she convinced herself that with enough penitence she could persuade God to forgive her for losing her virginity two months before the wedding.

Cheryl grimaced as she recalled how terrified she had been in the days and weeks that followed, fearful that she might have become pregnant that night. Her mother would have been able to do the math easily enough had Cheryl started showing signs.

She slipped her hand down now under her pyjama bottoms

and lightly massaged her uterus. It was indeed irritated from last night.

Worrying all that time, when I could have been just relishing the joy of marrying my quiet, loveable high school sweetheart, she scolded herself. It was pathetically needless anxiety, as her doctor had later confirmed. For the five years of their marriage, she and Rob had tried to have a baby—so much lovemaking in this bed, thrilling initially and then increasingly desperate as their effort bore no fruit. Cheryl continued to soothe with her fingers that life-creating centre which for her could never create a life.

And then there was that morning when she'd reached over to cuddle Rob before they both had to get up for work and discovered a cold, grey corpse usurping the place of her 28-year-old husband with his never-detected faulty heart.

Moving incrementally, she wrapped her arms around her pillow and buried her head as deeply as possible. A few twitches betrayed her muted sobs, not loud enough to wake Trevor. She took hold of the edge of the pillowcase and wiped her eyes. She studied the lumpy pillow. *I could get new ones at the same time I get a new bed,* she thought. *If I get a new bed.*

Trevor would object, even if she were buying it with her own money. "What's wrong with this one?" he'd demand to know. And she couldn't think of a way to explain herself that wouldn't involve some reference to Rob or some implied complaint about Trevor. During her initial rebound affair with Trevor, when she sought escape from her grief in his sexual potency, he had been respectful. It was her house after all. But that was a small detail dismissed early on as inconsequential. For the past six years, it had been their house, sometimes even his house—a proprietary attitude that extended beyond the physical belongings to include her time and her body.

Cheryl knew she couldn't get back to sleep now. Once she started fretting, she was awake for the day. Cautiously, she lifted up the sheet and comforter, slipped her right leg out, and pivoted her body around on her bum until she was sitting on the edge of the bed with both feet on the floor. She paused and listened for any change in his breathing. She didn't turn around to look at him, nervous that if she had wakened him, he would pin her with those glowering eyes, an inevitable prelude to either a morning beating or morning sex. Or both.

The bed creaked as she lifted her weight off it and stood up facing the window. She didn't move for almost a minute to ensure that he remained asleep. Looking through the sheers, she could see the streetlight reflecting off the roof of the truck and illuminating the interior cab with an amber glow. She took a few steps toward the window. No, that wasn't from the street lamp. He had left the light on inside the cab, probably when he was fiddling with his music. *Oh, is he ever going to be pissed if it has drained the battery.* She smiled to herself. *But probably that's too small a light to cause a problem for the behemoth that sits menacingly in the driveway.* Her smile dissipated.

Without glancing back toward the bed, she tiptoed over to the closet and reached under the afghan on the shelf to retrieve her book. Clutching it to her breast, she shuffled out of the bedroom and gently pulled the door shut, turning the knob before it was quite closed, and then releasing it once it was. She moved down the hallway and used the toilet in the powder room near the front door.

Cheryl sat at the kitchen table, her hands resting palms down on the opened Cheyenne Library copy of *The Constant Gardener.* Over and over, her baby fingers flicked down along the edges of the book, at times with a vigorous tap as they hit the table, at other times lovingly caressing past the pages read and the yet-to-be-tackled ones. A periwinkle patterned cup and saucer—the set a wedding gift from a lifetime ago—sat next to the book, the tea barely touched, a light scum forming on the surface.

Cheryl saw only a gurney in the Nairobi morgue on which Tessa's body lay, covered by a sheet darkened with dried bloodstains and besieged by a persistent cluster of flies. Justin had uncovered her head to identify the body.

A series of waking coughs rumbled down the hallway from the bedroom and plodded into the kitchen. Cheryl hadn't made Trevor's coffee yet. She glanced up at the percolator sitting on the counter and then over toward the cupboard door, behind which rested the large tin of Maxwell House. She sat quietly. She turned down a corner on the page, closed the book, and ran her fingers along the spine. Her teeth squeezed lightly the interior folds of her cheeks and ridges of her lips. Her jaw muscles remained taut for a few moments and then gently released. She became aware of her breathing—it was measured and calm, no nervous palpitations.

"Coffee, CC." Trevor's voice was garbled, partly muted by the pillow he would have positioned over his head to ward off the morning sun.

Cheryl lifted her hands from the book and placed them slowly around the edges of the kitchen table, one on each side. She wrapped her fingers underneath the lip and tightened her grip.

"CC?" This time he spoke more distinctly.

"Morning, Dear," Cheryl said, turning her head toward the hallway. She noted, with surprise, that her voice had not quivered.

"For God's sake, where's my coffee, CC?"

Cheryl took three deep breaths, tightened her grip further on the sides of the table, shuttered her eyes tightly, and said as matter-of-factly as she could muster, "Don't you remember, Dear? You said you'd make it this morning."

"Fuck you!" Commotion noise came from the bedroom. Cheryl could envisage the pillow tossed off the bed toward the upholstered chair, landing on top of the crumpled sweatshirt, and then slipping down onto the jeans and boxers and socks on the floor, the sheet and comforter thrust aside as Trevor stumbled out of bed, one hand covering his eyes and the other arm outstretched in front to help keep him from bumping into the dresser on his way toward the bathroom door. A moment later, the sound of a powerful stream of pee hit the toilet bowl, spasmodically. The rim and the floor beneath were getting watered as well. She waited to hear the flush. There was no flush.

Cheryl opened her eyes, released her security grip, brought her arms back up onto the table, and reopened the book. She fixed her gaze on a page that she had chosen randomly, practicing an intent reading pose.

Trevor walked into the kitchen and cuffed the back of her head as he passed behind her on his way to the counter.

"Ouch. I wish you wouldn't do that," Cheryl said quietly without looking up from the jumble of letters on the page.

"I weeshh you woodn't doo thaaat," Trevor lisped. He yanked open the cupboard door and grabbed the coffee can. "What the fuck's gotten into you lately?" He pulled the lid off the percolator and dropped it with a clang on the counter. After prying off the plastic lid of the coffee tin, he upended it and tapped it against the top of the pot, spilling grounds, some of which ended up in the basket. He placed the percolator under the tap, opened the faucet for a few moments, and then set the percolator back down on the counter. Cheryl snuck a peak, smiled to herself, and said nothing. He put the lid back on and plugged in the machine.

Turning around, he leaned against the counter and glowered at her. She lifted her head and looked directly into his eyes for a few moments. And then, as calmly as possible, she let her gaze drift down his body to his yellow-stained boxers. Trevor followed the path of her eyes. He smirked. Grabbing a hold of his basket and giving it a vigorous shake, he said, "Aha. Getting ready for a bit of morning delight, are you, Babes?"

Cheryl smiled back at him.

"Wantin' more? That's it, right?" he said. That was so far from it, but Cheryl played along, not responding but looking down at her hands, which were resting on top of the book.

She stopped smiling and took a deep breath. Looking up at him, she said slowly, "Trevor, I think it's perhaps time you started looking for your own place."

———— ⁓ ————

Cheryl had held it together so far—ignoring the stare of the gas jockey when she stopped for a fill-up, nodding nonchalantly to Ray as she swung past him in the office foyer, pretending not to notice Mr. Slate's hesitant approach, retreat, approach, retreat, as she hung up her coat and took her seat at her desk. Patty came breezing in a few minutes later, chatting up a storm with everyone in the office. Six feet from their shared desk, she froze in her tracks, gobsmacked by the sight of Cheryl's face. At that point, Cheryl lost it, tears streaming down her face, sobs loud enough to attract attention from the outer office. Cheryl buried her head amongst the papers on her desk, one hand covering her waterworks eyes and the other arm flying up instinctively and wrapping around the back of her head.

The defensive posture told Patty everything she needed to know.

Patty cradled Cheryl's shoulders and watched her in the mirror of the women's washroom, trying valiantly to reconstruct the makeup camouflage over the bruises, the soggy tissue disintegrating in her hand and leaving streak marks across her friend's cheeks. "Here, let me see what I can do," Patty said, turning Cheryl's face toward her. She reached up into her purse on the shelf above the sink and rummaged through it until she came up with her compact. "Ta-da!"

"The weekend was hell," Cheryl said quietly.

Patty opened her compact and raised the blush applicator up toward the blue-black skin around Cheryl's eyes. "Don't talk, Dearie," Patty cautioned as she started to dab at Cheryl's face. "Just let me make you pretty again."

Cheryl let out a wail, pushed Patty away, knocking her against the hard enamel sink, turned on her heels, and tumbled into one of the stalls, collapsing onto the floor and retching into the toilet bowl. Patty put one hand on the sink to steady herself and rubbed her bruised hip with the other. She watched the crumpled figure on the floor in the stall until the vomiting seemed exhausted and was replaced by a quiet whimpering. Entering the stall, Patty unrolled a large handful of toilet paper, raised Cheryl's face upward, and wiped the lingering spittle off her chin. She rolled the paper up into a tight ball and clenched it in her fist.

"Cheryl, Baby," Patty said as she opened her fist and displayed the toilet paper ball. "This is what we do with shit like your Trevor." Patty dropped the paper into the toilet bowl, raised her stiletto up onto the flushing lever, and pushed down, sending the water, vomit, and paper plummeting into Cheyenne's sewer system. Then she pushed it again three times. "For good measure, my dearie." Cheryl looked back and forth between the toilet bowl and Patty's hard-set jaw and flaming eyes. She lifted her hand off the floor and placed it on top of Patty's foot, which was still resting on the flushing lever. Pushing down gently, she activated another flush. She pushed again. Now looking up at Patty, Cheryl started to giggle. Patty helped Cheryl to her feet. Leaning against the stall divider, Patty wrapped her arms around Cheryl and hugged tightly. Cheryl flinched a couple of times before relaxing and burying her face in the cashmere sweater.

Patty and Cheryl walked arm in arm out of the washroom, Patty with her head up and shoulders back and with a facial expression that telegraphed to all their colleagues, "She'll be okay. Just don't ask her anything about what's happened, and for God's sake, don't gawk at her bruises." Cheryl, eyes sporadically glancing around but mostly downcast, and lips quivering despite a resolute intention to exude confidence, headed slowly toward her desk, leaning heavily on Patty's arm. They settled into their respective chairs and turned on their computers. The hush that had descended on the office—part embarrassed, part respectful—gave way to the customary tapping of keyboards, answering of telephones, opening of envelopes, swearing at bureaucratic glitches, laughing at each other's lame jokes, and engaging in general chitchat to relieve the paper-shuffling tedium that constituted much of their workdays.

Cheryl was grateful for that tedium. Generally, she resented the boredom of her clerical job, but today it was a gift. She mechanically went about the data entry work; it was so routine, she didn't have to concentrate. And yet, it required just enough attention to squeeze the weekend images out of her mind—a perfect combination of distraction and minimal energy requirement.

The morning hours passed. Patty kept up her half of their customary banter, generously absolving Cheryl of having to respond. At one point, Patty mimicked a typical Cheryl comment, feigning both sides of their jesting. Cheryl looked over and smiled in appreciation. As the noon hour approached, her anxiety rose. Going to the lunchroom would require interaction with others and the usual sort of how-was-your-weekend conversations.

But, as it happened, this was not to be one of the usual noon hours in the lunchroom.

Trevor had been sitting in his truck in the parking lot for more than an hour. He kept the volume on his radio turned low. Slouched down, his figure was almost invisible, absorbed into the high-backed seat and obscured by the dark tint of the windows and the interior condensation that fogged their surface. None of the social security clientele who had walked into the building from the bus stop, or those who had driven in and parked their cars near his truck, gave any indication of having noticed him.

Arranged on the seat beside him were the photographs and newspaper clippings that he had torn off their bedroom wall before leaving the house, the framed picture of him and Cheryl taken two years ago at the Laramie County Fair, and the public library copy of *The Constant Gardener* with three bullet holes clear through it, and a sap-stained back cover where it had been jostled against the Rocky Mountain juniper during this morning's target practice. Nestled on the passenger's-side floor and covered with a tarp stained from years of wrapping killed game was his .44 Remington Magnum rifle.

The Smith and Wesson Special lay in his lap. Of all the decisions that he had wrestled with this morning, which handgun to bring had been the most problematic. It had to be just right. Trevor wrapped his hand around the handle and lifted the weapon, admiring the polished satin stainless steel finish, flexing his fingers along the comfortable synthetic grip, and checking the five rounds that rested snugly in the chambers. He moved the revolver down to between his legs and rubbed it along the inseam of his pants until he was hard. His erection extended three inches beyond the five-inch length of the gun's barrel. He had made the comparison on many occasions.

The clock on the dashboard read 11:19. He didn't have much longer to wait. Half past eleven had struck him as the perfect time to make his entrance. All the staff would be back from their morning coffee break, and no one would have left yet for lunch.

Cheryl would be at her desk for sure.

The media would have time to get their footage, interview witnesses, and file their stories before the deadline for the supper hour news broadcasts.

The digits flipped from 11:27 to 11:28.

Trevor turned off the radio. Holding the revolver in his left hand, he reached over and, with his right hand, drew the tarp off the rifle and lifted the gun up, dropping it on the seat, where it added a few more creases to the fading pictures and newspaper clippings. Picking up the framed photo, he held it very close to his face so he could see every detail, moved it farther away to capture the overall effect, and then brought it back in once more. Trevor placed his lips on Cheryl's laughing face. Noticing the mark his kiss had left on the glass, he shifted his thumb over to smudge it off, changed his mind, and left it. As he was placing the picture back down on the seat, the light from the overcast sky outside highlighted his own reflection on the glass covering the photo. He scowled. "Shit, I'm not looking my best," he grumbled.

11:29.

Picking up the rifle and laying the revolver in his lap, he grabbed hold of the door handle and thrust the door open. Holding one gun in each hand, he stepped out of the truck and pushed the door closed behind him with his bum. He headed toward the office building.

Ray stood at the urinal, waiting and waiting. *Damn prostate,* he thought. Finally, a slow dribble began, followed by a gradually increasing stream. It was never forceful anymore, but it was adequate and served the purpose. He shook, tucked it back in, zipped up, and moved to the sink to wash his hands. Just as he turned the faucet lever, a piercing squeal ricocheted around the room. He stared at the lever. The building management had replaced the previous leaky and rusting hardware that used to squeak. Ray turned the water off. He heard no comparable squeal as when he had turned it on. There was silence.

Ray jerked his head up. The room was too silent. Usually, the hubbub from the office could be heard in the washroom. But he heard no voices now. A phone rang, and then rang and rang. No one was answering the caller. Ray's internal security antenna shot up.

Tightening a grip on his holstered revolver, Ray tiptoed toward the door and placed a sweating palm on the handle. The door eased open without a sound, and Ray stepped out into the short hallway that led from the washroom into the main reception area. He would have to walk five or six steps and turn a corner before he could get a view. The phone had stopped ringing but then immediately started up again. Ray heard whimpering as well as the bloody insistent phone. But otherwise, all was silent—a-nothing-about-this-is-right silence.

Leaning against the wall just shy of the corner, Ray inched his head around it.

Trevor stood, feet apart, the rifle resting in the crook of his right arm, its muzzle pointed into the office. The revolver was in his left hand, which was outstretched at shoulder height. He had a finger on the trigger of each gun. Head perfectly still but eyes darting in every direction, he moved his arms slowly side to side so that one or the other was almost constantly trained on the clusters of people whom he had corralled together in groups. An elderly man on his knees mumbled through the rosary, tears streaming down his bowed head. A young woman held a fidgety baby, smothering the child's head in the folds of her ragged coat.

"Cheryl, get your ass out here," Trevor bellowed toward the Plexiglas door that led from the reception area into the administrative offices. There was no sound or sign of movement from the inner office. "Cheryl, for fuck's sake, I haven't got all day."

Mr. Slate's reedy voice emerged from behind the baffles. "Sir ... would you ... please put away ... your ... your ... weapons?"

"Fuck that shit. Send out Cheryl and you'll all be fine."

There was whispered commotion behind the door. Then more distinctly Slate could be heard saying, "No, no, don't ..."

The plexiglass door flew open.

Out strode Patty, one hand fiercely planted on her hip, the other trailing behind her and clasping the hand of Cheryl, who walked in stride but with less conviction. "You're going to have to deal with me first, you shithead," Patty yelled at Trevor.

Trevor stepped back a pace and looked Patty up and down. He craned his head to the side and focused on Cheryl. "This is the sidekick you talk about, Cheryl? I had no idea she was such a babe."

"Babe schmabe. Forget about me, you asshole. What the fuck do you think you're doing riding in like Wild Bill Hickok after my girl here?"

Trevor's eyes fairly bulged out of his head. "Your girl? Are you two lezzies?"

"Don't you just wish," Patty spit out.

Cheryl stepped forward slightly. Patty jerked her clasped hand to reel her back. "It's okay, Patty," Cheryl said. "This is for me to deal with."

Cheryl turned, looked directly at Trevor, and took two hesitant steps toward him. "This is no way to handle things Trev," she said quietly.

Trevor's breathing quickened and his hands started to quiver. "I'm sorry, CC," he said softly. "This is the only way. Stop there. No closer."

Trevor pointed the rifle directly at Cheryl and slowly raised the revolver barrel into his mouth.

Ray's shot hit Trevor's right hand. The rifle flew out of it. The revolver discharged into his mouth. Trevor's body crashed backward against a wall and then went down onto the floor. Cheryl screamed and fainted into Patty's arms.

References

Le Carré, John. *The Constant Gardener.* London: Hodder & Stoughton, 2001.

Proulx, Annie. "Brokeback Mountain" in *Close Range: Wyoming Stories.* New York: Scribner, 1999.

morgan and maurice

A PINCH ON THE BUM IS AN UNUSUAL INSPIRATION for a novel. But that was the case with E. M. Forster's *Maurice*.

Edward Morgan Forster was born in London on January 1, 1879. His father died of consumption when Morgan was only 11 years old. The boy then lived with his widowed mother, Lily, more or less consistently until her death in 1945. Morgan acquiesced to her wishes in almost all things. Lily chose the residences in which they lived, the destinations to which they travelled together, and the company they visited—mostly relatives and widowed women like her. By outward appearances, it was an amiable, loving relationship. Privately, Morgan chafed at their mutual dependence. In his diaries, he castigated himself for not having greater independence of spirit.

Morgan was an adolescent at the time of the infamous 1895 trial of Oscar Wilde. The tragic outcome for Wilde within a context of social antagonism toward "deviants" reinforced Morgan's predisposition to secrecy. He was a quiet, reserved, studious youth—the polar opposite to Wilde's flamboyance. His life as a student at King's College, Cambridge, brought him into contact with a community of men who were adventurous in their intellectual, artistic, literary, and sexual lives. But Morgan remained in the background, always observing. Lytton Strachey nicknamed him the Taupe (mole). John Maynard Keynes saw him as "the elusive colt of a dark horse." To Leonard Woolf's eye, he was "strange, elusive, evasive."

After finishing his degree at Cambridge, Morgan wrote, observed, wrote, looked after his mother, wrote, travelled, and wrote. By the age of 34 in 1913, he had become a significant literary figure in England, the author of many short stories and the critically acclaimed novels *Where Angels Fear to Tread* and *Howard's End*.

He was also still a virgin bereft of any sexual experience save a minor prepubescent incident.

With years of homoerotic dreams and fantasies, Morgan was reconciled to being homosexual, albeit without having had any opportunity to act on it. He quietly socialized with other gay men but remained fiercely closeted in his family and public life. He never explicitly acknowledged his sexual orientation to his mother.

While Forster was visiting the country home of the aged writer Edward Carpenter in the fall of 1913, Carpenter's working-class lover flirtatiously pinched Morgan's buttocks. The erotic charge from the strong man's touch so energized Morgan that it broke a repressive dam in his literary imagination. He saw in his mind's eye an entire outline for a novel—plot, characters, and all. Over the next two years, he wrote *Maurice*, now canonized as one of the great early gay novels in the English language.

And then he essentially buried it. *Maurice* remained unpublished for almost 60 years, only being released, according to Forster's wishes, after he had died.

⌐‿⌐

When Morgan was 11 years old, he was sent to his first school, having been tutored at home up to this point. The Kent House School in Eastbourne had only thirty students, all boys. Morgan was miserable. He was separated from his mother for the first time in his life and was mocked by the other boys for his shyness and his diminutive stature. One day in the showers, a student declared to the others, "Have you seen Forster's cock? A beastly little brown thing."

Being poor in sports, he was excused in the second term from playing games and given permission to spend the time wandering on his own along the Downs for exercise. On one such occasion in March 1891, he encountered a 40- or 50-year-old man peeing into the brush. The man invited Morgan to come over and sit with him. The man then unzipped his own pants again, took out his penis, and told Morgan to fondle it. Morgan obeyed. In short order, the man attained an erection and came, or as Forster wrote years later in his *Sex Diaries*, "Some thick white droplets trickled out." The man offered Morgan a shilling, which the lad declined, and then bid goodbye. "He didn't try to handle me," Morgan wrote, "and I went off quietly."

Initially, Morgan wasn't troubled by the incident. But as he returned to school, he became distressed about whether he should tell anyone. He sensed that it would prompt a strong reaction if he did so. He eventually decided to write about it to his mother. That letter unleashed a chain of events involving family, clergy, the school, and the police. The blundering response of the headmaster left a particularly strong impression on Morgan. The man he had encountered was never identified and the affair was dropped. To Morgan, the intense reaction of others was out of all proportion to the incident. Morgan concluded that he could no longer confide with confidence in his mother and that he should keep silent about private matters.

Such Victorian awkwardness on sexual matters gets treated with comic finesse by Forster in the opening chapter of *Maurice* when Maurice's teacher, Mr. Ducie, attempts an elementary sex education lesson with Maurice by drawing pictograms with a stick in the sand during a school beach outing.

It was at King's College, Cambridge, that Morgan fell in love for the first time.

He entered university in the fall of 1897 at the age of 18, looking forward to the intellectual stimulation but dreading the necessity of interacting with other people. He was spindly and gawky, shy and insecure. He was certainly intelligent, but that gave him little self-confidence, because he wasn't aware of his gifts. To escape the pressure, he took to riding a bicycle through the town and into the countryside. That way he could be alone.

By his second year, Morgan had settled in more comfortably and made the effort to become more social. To his delight, he found it reciprocated. He was assigned a set of rooms on the top floor of the comfortable Bodley's Building, recently built in a Gothic style to fit in architecturally with the older buildings. One of his housemates was Hugh Owen Meredith (known to his peers by his initials, HOM), a young man who exuded the overtly virile qualities that Morgan felt he lacked. HOM had dashingly good looks, athleticism, and self-confidence, and he fused these effortlessly with brilliant intellectual capacity, to which Morgan could relate. As if there were any further kindling needed to fuel Morgan's attraction, HOM proclaimed himself an atheist shortly after the two of them had met, vociferously rejecting traditional religious tenets just as Morgan had begun to do more circumspectly.

Confronted with Meredith's intelligence, attractiveness, and disposition, Morgan swooned. And to Morgan's delight, Meredith seemed to like him. For the first time in his life, Morgan had a real friend. The relationship was to prove less reciprocal than Morgan fantasized; in particular, it never became sexual. But in a way, that intensified the depth of Morgan's feelings. The agony of an affection that was at once encouraged and rebuffed plays out in the tortured connection between Maurice and his long-term love interest Clive Durham in the novel that was still 15 years away from being written.

In the rarefied atmosphere of the King's College student body, the ancient Greek history of male bonding became for Morgan the philosophical and spiritual model for deep homoerotic friendship. But unlike in classical Athenian society, subterfuge cloaked male-to-male physical relationships, perhaps a recoiling after the disgrace into which Oscar Wilde's trial a few years earlier had cast public homosexuality. In a wickedly funny scene in *Maurice*, Forster describes the aversion that reigned in the Cambridge environment to any explicit acknowledgment:

> They attended the Dean's translation class, and when one of the men was forging quietly ahead Mr. Cornwallis observed in a flat toneless voice: "Omit: a reference to the unspeakable vice of the Greeks."

In a conversation between Clive and Maurice that follows the class, Clive scoffs at the Dean's squeamishness and accuses him of academic hypocrisy:

> I regard it as a point of pure scholarship. The Greeks, or most of them, were that way inclined, and to omit it is to omit a mainstay of Athenian society.

Forster then writes the following:

> No more was said at the time, but he [Maurice] was free of another subject, and one that he had never mentioned to any living soul. He hadn't known that it could be mentioned, and when Durham did so in the middle of the sunlit court a breath of liberty touched him.

Such a casual reference to homosexuality by the object of his affection quickened Maurice's heart. But just as candid conversations between Morgan and HOM were never to materialize into intimate relations, so Maurice is to be frustrated by Clive's insistence that their love remain platonic.

———⌣———

In the summer of 1901, Morgan slipped from the robust fraternity of his Cambridge friends back into a desolate sorority with his mother and her female companions.

Surprisingly, Morgan had not done terribly well scholastically and ended his degree with mediocre grades insufficient to allow further study at the university. He considered taking training to become a teacher. The Cambridge don was not encouraging. Morgan's fantasy of becoming a writer had been stoked by a few short stories that had been published in periodicals. A small inheritance from an aunt provided the option for an extended period of travel that he felt would give him time, inspiration, and material for further writing.

Of course, his mother, Lily, would have to come along.

In October they set off for Italy. On one level, the trip was a disaster. Morgan had researched every museum, church, art gallery, and historic site that they should visit, but he was constantly getting them lost, losing his maps and guidebooks, and missing their train connections. In January he sprained his ankle, and a few weeks later fell on the steps of St. Peter's and broke his arm, rendering him dependent on his mother for almost everything, including bathing. Lily nagged him for his incompetence, reprimands that Morgan quietly accepted as justified.

The inspiration that Morgan had anticipated Italy would offer was being smothered under the stress and dreariness of his responsibility for his mother. He was awed by the richness of Italian culture, but he couldn't summon the creative energy to translate it into satisfactory narrative. He tried writing but found what he produced too pedestrian. The misadventures and disappointments left him despondent.

That all changed as the warmth of spring broke over him in Naples. He suddenly found himself with a charged homoerotic dream life and a stimulated writing imagination.

The intensity of the nocturnal dreams caught him by surprise, a pleasant surprise to be sure. At the time, he chose not to analyse them but simply to enjoy them. But their impact spilled from night's slumber into daytime consciousness and led to a burst of creativity.

One lovely May morning, he was out walking by himself in the hills near Ravello. The sun was shining and a light breeze was wafting through the trees, the town picturesquely visible far below, set off against the deep blue of the Tyrrhenian Sea. And then suddenly, there it was in his mind's eye—a fully formed idea for what would become his "Story of a Panic." Decades later he would describe as follows:

> I sat down in a valley, a few miles above the town, and suddenly the first chapter of the story rushed into my mind as if it had waited for me there. I received it as an entity and wrote it out as soon as I returned to the hotel.

"Story of a Panic" integrates classical themes, specifically those of Ovid's *Metamorphosis*, into a narrative about a group of bourgeois English tourists in the Italian countryside being traumatized by an encounter with some sort of bacchanalian presence. Rushing back to their hotel, they realize that the youngest member of the group, Eustace, is missing. They eventually find him altered almost beyond recognition, robust and enlivened apparently by the sensuous spirit of Pan. Eustace amorously embraces the attractive Italian waiter at the hotel, to the horror of the others.

After Morgan and Lily returned to England in September 1902, Morgan showed the story to Cambridge friends. Charles Sayle and Maynard Keynes immediately read a homosexual subtext into it. Morgan was horrified by their interpretation and rejected it out of hand as lascivious and mean-spirited. It was only years later that Morgan was prepared to acknowledge that there was merit in their perceptions: "I had been excited as I wrote and the passages where Sayle had thought something was up had excited me the most."

Over time, Morgan came to appreciate more and more how significant sexual energy was as a driver of his creative imagination. But he was never comfortable in being particularly explicit about that "sacred and mysterious force."

As he and his mother settled back into life in English society in the fall of 1902, Morgan struggled with the interrelated dilemmas of discerning whom he was as a person, what he would do professionally, and what it would mean for his life being sexually attracted to men. It was a struggle that he conducted primarily in solitude. He took up a part-time position teaching at the Working Men's College. He was relieved to have something concrete to do, and he enjoyed being in the company of energetic, virile young men. Furthermore, his Cambridge heterosexual flame Hugh Meredith was living nearby the college and actively sought out Morgan's company and friendship. Going through a protracted emotional depression of his own, HOM found Morgan to be the one person in whom he could find solace. HOM told Maynard Keynes, "I think I am dead really now ... [but] I come to life temporarily when I meet Forster." Morgan relished their time together despite the frustrations of its chaste nature.

His sexual life was one of "abstinence," as he referred to it, as a function of his own timidity and for fear of upsetting his mother. The question for him was how he could understand his heart's longing in ways that felt authentic.

There were models around that struck him as fundamentally

inauthentic, at least as ways to describe his aspirations. Not for him was the emerging medical description of "inversion" coming from British sexologist Havelock Ellis and his counterparts in Germany. And Morgan recoiled from the open flamboyancy of the type personified by Oscar Wilde, Lytton Strachey, and Charles Sayle. In his diaries, Morgan adopted the term *minority* to depict his position. What he sought, and what was to become a fundamental theme in his writing, was "the search for an honest connection with another human being." His ideal for his own life—and what he felt should be accessible to other members of this minority—was to find the kind of intimacy, love, and domesticity that was the societal norm for the majority.

He was clear about something else. Though the prospects of an active sexual life were minimal, the capacity of his imagination was unlimited. He could write.

In terms of intimacy, Morgan's sexual life continued on for years as a wasteland. Not so his emotional life. And one or the other, or both, stimulated his pen.

In a real-world echo of his fictional "Story of a Panic," he encountered a shepherd boy while walking one summer day in 1904 through the Wiltshire countryside near Salisbury. What followed was an innocent 15 minutes of quiet conversation about "nothing—still one of my favourite subjects." Yet, the connection left him "charged with emotion … in that juncture of mind and heart where the creative impulse sparks." The shepherd boy became the model for the character of Stephen Wonham in *The Longest Journey*, Forster's novel that is replete with ambiguous homoeroticism and a subtle moral subtext to be true to oneself.

While writing *The Longest Journey*, another sexually charged yet sexually barren relationship exploded into Morgan's life reminiscent of what he had experienced with HOM. Syed Ross

Masood was 17 years old, a decade younger than Morgan. He had come from India in 1906 to prepare for entrance exams to Oxford and was staying with a family who lived nearby Morgan and his mother. Morgan was enlisted to tutor him. Masood was tall, dark, and handsome, an exotic prince of an aristocratic Muslim family. He was heterosexual yet uninhibited in his expressions of affection to Morgan. Morgan fell deeply in love. Their intense relationship would endure for three decades, chaste despite the mutual protestations of love one for the other.

The glowing reviews that greeted the publication of *The Longest Journey* in April 1907 helped cement a contract for another novel. Forster returned to material that he had been working with years earlier, what he referred to as his "Lucy novel" after the main character and what was later to become *A Room with a View*. He was frustrated with what he perceived to be an arid tone in the draft. Walt Whitman came to his rescue, in a manner of speaking. Forster read Whitman's "Calamus" poems in *Leaves of Grass* and found in them an exuberance of life and sensuality for "the manly love of comrades." Forster launched into a reading of other literature that implicitly or explicitly celebrated male-to-male love, revisiting ancient Greek writings that he had encountered at Cambridge, poetry of Michelangelo, sonnets of Shakespeare, and Victorian and Edwardian novels. Returning to his work in progress, he hit upon an idea of suggesting a possible sexual misconduct of one of the characters as a trigger for the developing plot. The veracity of the perceived assault remains unresolved in the novel, but its sexual nature, though clearly heterosexual, seems to have been prompted in Forster's mind through his reading of Whitman and others. *A Room with a View* was well received by critics and the public when it came out.

Early in 1908, Morgan had an opportunity to meet Henry James through mutual acquaintances. With great anticipation, he went to tea at the proscribed hour, looking forward to an afternoon of stimulating conversation with another homosexual writer. James was 66, heavy-set, and balding. Morgan was 27, was shy, and stammered. James mistook him for someone else from King's College. Morgan was too flustered to correct him. James held forth in what struck Morgan as a pretentious faux English-nobility manner. The meeting was a great disappointment to Morgan. But the day's adventures were not to be over as he left James's residence that afternoon. As he walked down the lane away from Lamb House, he saw in the distance a workman heading home and pausing to light a cigarette. The light of the flame flashed through the dusky late afternoon and struck Morgan like a shot. He went home and, in his diary, penned an erotic poem that contrasted the austere house of high art in which he had spent the afternoon with the potent energy of real-world male sexuality. Morgan could write about desire. He just couldn't find it within himself to act on it.

A trauma the following year compounded his sexual anxiety. He was invited to participate in the festivities surrounding the marriage of Malcolm Darling, one of his King's College friends. On Thursday night, July 8, 1909, Morgan accompanied Darling to dinner, where he was introduced to the affable Ernest Merz, who was Darling's best friend and was to be his groomsman at the wedding. After dinner, Darling headed home and Morgan walked Merz back to Merz's fashionable apartment near the Royal Academy, where they said goodbye and parted. The next morning Merz's body was found. He had hung himself. The death was not only traumatic for the circle of friends but also seemingly inexplicable. No one had perceived an inkling of distress in Merz's demeanour. In the following days, Darling speculated to Morgan that Merz might have been homosexual. Morgan sought to comfort him but felt that such efforts would be sabotaged if he admitted to Darling that he himself was homosexual. He felt trapped, and watched as the prospect of living more openly and honestly disappeared further into a misty future.

Forster's reading of Walt Whitman had not only liberated him to rework *A Room with a View* more to his satisfaction but also evoked an idea for another novel. He set to work. When *Howard's End* came out in October 1910, the critics were nearly unanimous in their praise, calling Forster "one of the great novelists" and "one of the handful of writers who count." He appreciated the literary affirmation and felt more liberated of his dependence on his mother by the money that his book sales generated, but he was not enamoured by the celebrity status that accompanied his success. He felt nostalgic for his previous obscurity. He lusted after the beautiful men whom he would see in daily life and felt tormented by their inaccessibility. After Morgan casually commented on the attractiveness of a charming boy while lunching at the Savile, a member of the elite club who was a total stranger to Morgan threatened him with blackmail. At least that's how Morgan interpreted the interaction.

The monies from the sales of *Howard's End* opened up the possibility of more travel for Morgan. He hoped a trip would stimulate him out of the creative fallow period into which he had once again slipped. The object of his affection, Syed Ross Masood, had returned to India, as had Morgan's Cambridge friend Malcolm Darling, who served in the Indian Civil Service. Morgan launched himself onto his first voyage to India from the fall of 1912 to the spring of 1913, not only seeing many of the sights of the subcontinent but also studying the dynamics of imperialism in the relationships between the British and the Indians, a theme that he was to explore artistically in the next decade as he wrote *A Passage to India*. Morgan spent as much time as possible with Masood, who arranged portions of his travel, introduced him to colourful personalities who would find their images penned into *A Passage to India*, and helped him negotiate the complexities of Indian life amongst the varied classes and castes.

The trip was important for Morgan, but it did not have the hoped-for impact in liberating his artistic creativity or relieving his sexual frustration. Back in England, he began sketching out a possible novel based in India, but the writing did not come easily. He would procrastinate by taking long walks around London, his erotic fantasies leading him to loiter in Hyde Park or near public lavatories, barely letting himself hope for possible sexual connections. They never happened. In June 1913, he took in a performance of Nijinsky dancing almost naked in *L'Après-midi d'un faune* at Covent Garden, and found himself aroused yet despondent at the contrast between Nijinsky's exhibitionism and his own sexual and literary inhibitions. Morgan recorded in his diary that the dancer portrayed "a humorous and alarming animal, free from the sentimentality of my stories."

But Morgan's despondency was to be rattled to the core with the opportunity in September 1913 to visit the writer Edward Carpenter and his robust young lover at their home in Millthorpe, the visit that led directly to the creation of *Maurice*.

———

Edward Carpenter was almost 70 when Morgan made his pilgrimage to meet him. Having come from aristocratic stock, Carpenter had early in life jettisoned the trappings of his class and committed himself to writing and to social reform movements. He considered becoming an Anglican priest but chose instead to carve his own path, one unencumbered by institutional expectations. He took up residence in slum areas of Sheffield and advocated for equality of the classes, women's rights, and the eradication of prejudice against homosexuals. Carpenter visited, and slept with, Walt Whitman in America and composed Whitmanesque poetry exulting in "homogenic love." Among his admirers and devotees were counted George Bernard Shaw, William Morris, and Goldie and Roger Fry.

And he practiced what he preached. Carpenter lived openly for almost 40 years with his working-class lover, George Merrill, in their modest rural cottage, where they subsisted frugally, grew much of their own food, and welcomed visitors. Though the pretence of Morgan's visit was to share ideas with a fellow literary figure, it was the opportunity to witness firsthand Carpenter's and Merrill's open and loving long-term homosexual relationship that was his real agenda.

Morgan enjoyed his conversations in the cottage kitchen with Carpenter, but it was the dark, handsome Merrill's clandestine groping of Morgan's buttocks that stimulated him physically and artistically. Morgan had never experienced an erotic encounter of that intensity. Fifty years later he was still relishing the charge: "It was as much psychological as physical. It seemed to go straight through the small of my back into my ideas, without involving any thoughts."

And the idea that it germinated was to write a love story that involved two "ordinary affectionate" men who, rather than succumbing to a tragic end, would work their way through their differences of class and the prejudices of society to end in each other's arms and spend the rest of their lives together, happily. That is what makes the novel *Maurice* groundbreaking and radical.

In Forster's words, "I was determined that in fiction anyway two men should fall in love and remain in it for the ever and ever that fiction allows."

The principle characters in the novel are Maurice Hall; his university colleague Clive Durham, to whom Maurice is deeply attracted but who does not, or will not, allow himself to reciprocate; and Alec Scudder, a gamekeeper on Durham's estate with whom, against all social odds, Maurice falls in love, and who responds in kind.

Forster's intention in writing *Maurice* was that it would be for his eyes only. On completion, though, he decided to share it with a few confidants. Their reactions were mixed. On occasion over the decades, he would haul it out and tinker with various sections. But he refused to consider releasing it while he was alive—publishing it would be unthinkable, he wrote in his diary, "until my death and England's."

Through the midwifery of Morgan's friend and protégé Christopher Isherwood, *Maurice* finally saw the light of day in 1971—a year after Morgan's death and at a time when English society was finally transitioning to a more open acceptance of homosexuality.

Writers draw on what they know. They also make things up. Forster did both in *Maurice*.

Epilogue: Maurice and Morgan in Conversation

We're on the cover of the current *GLR*, in the running for title as the first modern gay novel. As if there were any question.

What's *GLR*?

The *Gay and Lesbian Review*. Literary new and views. Oh yes, there's the little matter of you having died 25 years before they started publishing. Sorry.

What's our competition?

Excuse me?

Catch up, boy. What other novels are they considering for first "gay" novel?

Oh, let me see. Oscar Wilde's *The Picture of Dorian Gray* ...

A good piece of work, admittedly, but hardly an overtly "gay" novel. I'm glad that I never met Wilde. If I was so timid having tea with doughty old Henry James, image how tongue-tied I'd have been with Wilde. Oh my, my, my. I shudder at the thought.

Proust's *Swann's Way* …

You're jesting. Magnificent writer that Proust was, but he was far too circumspect to tackle man-to-man love explicitly. Not like I did, at least.

Giovanni's Room, James Baldwin's 1956 novel, and, of course, your dear friend and protégé Christopher Isherwood's *A Single Man* that came out in 1964.

But these were written a generation after I wrote *Maurice*.

Yes, but they were published before *Maurice*.

There's also Gore Vidal's 1948 *The Pillar and the City* …

Vidal? That pompous hypocrite. He never acknowledged that there was such a thing as a man's love for another man as an inherent orientation. He'd only countenance that we were men participating in sexual acts with other men.

You're on thin ice accusing another gay author of hypocrisy.

Are you never going to let that go?

I might never have seen the light of day if it weren't for Isherwood publishing me after you died.

You existed as soon as I conceived of you the weekend that I spent with Edward and George, as soon as I fleshed you out in manuscript over the following months …

Don't be disingenuous.

Did I give you such a sophisticated vocabulary?

You really are a pompous ass sometimes.

Now, that's more the Maurice I know and love.

What I meant, as you well understand, is that I didn't exist in the imagination of the reading public all those long decades while you suppressed us—Clive, Alec, and me.

I didn't suppress you. I chose not to publish you. There's a difference.

Not from where I sit. Your fear of publishing *Maurice* looks to a lot of people like a case of being thoroughly ensconced in the closet, as the moderns say.

Oh, that is so unfair. And absolutely inaccurate.

Maybe a bit unfair, but not inaccurate. Don't you think being closeted is an appropriate explanation for why you never came out to Lily or wanted her to know anything about *Maurice*?

Leave Mother out of this.

When Joe Ackerley was trying to convince you to publish *Maurice*, he used André Gide as an example. Gide had published his Socratic dialogue defense of homosexuality *Corydon*, as well as his explicit diary *Si le grain ne meurt*, which describes, amongst many other gems, cruising for young men in Morocco with Oscar Wilde. You shut down the discussion with Joe by blurting, "But Gide hasn't got a mother!"

Yes, well, he didn't. Anymore.

And even after Lily died in 1945 you refused to publish us.

England wasn't ready for a love story between two men, that is, one that ended happily.

You supported human rights campaigns for various oppressed minorities including homosexuals, especially as your fame and stature increased. But you never publicly identified yourself as homosexual—a "gay man," as is now the accepted nomenclature. You thought publishing *Maurice* would blow your cover?

You young people think everything is so simple.

That's a good one, accusing me of being simplistic after the complexities of life you penned for me.

What I mean is that I didn't cower in the shadows. I associated with many well-known homosexuals—Isherwood, Auden, Paul Cadmus, Glenway Westcott. For heaven's sake, I virtually lived with Benjamin Britten and Peter Pears while writing the libretto for *Billy Budd.*

Precisely my point. All of them were creating art that celebrated man-to-man love, and they were living that life openly …

As was I for so long with Bob Buckingham, the love of my life, even after he married May. And then after Robin was born, whose middle name was Morgan, I would remind you, the three of us essentially raised him together. When Robin was diagnosed with Hodgkin's disease and started to wither away, I sat with him for hours, gently stroking his hand. His death was the greatest tragedy of my life. He was Bob's and my child. Bob's and May's and my child.

All the more reason why you should have had the courage to publish *Maurice*, the one time you wrote about homosexual love.

Ah, my dear boy, you have always been obtuse. You can't help it. I have only myself to blame.

Don't patronize me.

For the perceptive souls within the reading public, they should have been able to discern in my other works the nuanced treatment of the plight of homosexuals in an oppressive society—positing Rickie's struggle in *The Longest Journey* as a metaphor; the homoerotic scenes and the treatment of Lucy's sexual awakening, admittedly heterosexual, in *A Room with a View*; characters with a "gay" sensibility, such as Cecil in *A Room with a View* and Freddy in *Howard's End*; the erotic dimensions in "Story of a Panic" …

The homosexual dynamics of which you only belatedly acknowledged, long after you had written it.

Yes, well, now you're being less obtuse. You're right that I didn't see what I was writing about in "Story of a Panic" until others thrust it in my face.

So, if you admit to having depicted homosexual characters and situations in these other, published works, it makes it all the more perplexing why you steadfastly refused to publish *Maurice* during your lifetime.

Remember your own biography, my dear boy. You are looking at life, and judging me harshly, by the standards of where you ended up— having found love and happiness with Alec. But you went through, or rather I put you through, quite a struggle before you got to that point, a struggle with religious orthodoxy; abusive encounters with medical authorities determined to ignore or, worse yet, cure you of your attraction to men; your own fears of losing social status or your job if it should become known that you were—how did you express it to Dr. Barry?—oh yes, "an unspeakable of the Oscar Wilde sort."

I certainly do remember all that, for God's sake. All you had to do was write it. I had to live it.

Yes, of course, I don't mean to minimize what you went through. But try to remember, I was writing it at a time when all those societal sanctions were dominant and ...

Yes?

Under the shadow ...

Go on, my dear Morgan. If you can't talk to me, to whom can you?

It was Oscar ... his trial ... his persecution ... we were all living under that shadow. Even though it happened almost 20 years before I wrote *Maurice*, his tragedy hung over all of us like an executioner's sword, ready to strike us down in a similarly ignominious manner.

I don't mean to be insensitive. I do realize how oppressive English society was at the time. But there were others who weren't cowered by the Wilde trauma. Lytton Strachey, for example, was part of your circle of friends at Cambridge. You used him as a model for my Cambridge acquaintance Risley.

And you'll recall what happened to Risley in the book—a fate not unlike Wilde's. For better or worse, I judged that it was not safe to publish a novel as explicit on the subject of man-to-man love as *Maurice* in the England of that day and age. And I take umbrage at your depiction of me as cowering under the Oscar Wilde legacy. I admit to being shy and awkward in life and intimidated at times by authority ...

Such as Lily ...

Okay, I'll grant you that … such as Mother … but I was never a cowerer. Oh dear, surely there is no such term as *cowerer*. Heavens, look how sloppily you've got me speaking.

You are so endearing when you get flustered.

If I were to point to a model of courage in those days, it wouldn't be Lytton Strachey. It would be Edward Carpenter … he and George Merrill living together openly for so many years despite the differences in their age and social class … making a home together in the country and so clearly loving each other. That's what I saw that weekend in September 1913 … that two men could find love together and live out that love for the rest of their lives. That was the inspiration for writing *Maurice*—the search for and achievement of an honest connection with another human being.

Not just George tweaking your buttocks?

Well, that was also a stimulation of sorts …

And in fact that depiction of yours of two men finding love and creating a happy life together is what you're being celebrated for in the *GLR* article. In their analysis, that's what makes us— well, *Maurice* specifically—revolutionary. They say that at the time you wrote *Maurice*, "there was no concept that same-sex love could form the basis of a stable and happy lifetime commitment, so Forster was genuinely innovative to imagine such a possibility."

"Genuinely innovative." Hmm. I rather like that accolade.

And when Isherwood arranged for it to be published in 1971 after you had died, it landed in the midst of the early days of the gay liberation movement, just a few years after the Stonewall riots.

The what?

You don't remember about the Stonewall bar in New York's Greenwich Village where drag queens and gay men fought back against police harassment for the first time, leading to days of rioting? I guess you were too far into your dotage years in your rooms at Cambridge …

I never had dotage years. I was cogent and articulate up to the end.

Yes, you were, more or less. But you may not have been following the news as keenly as in your earlier days. And to be fair, not many people realized at the time how pivotal the Stonewall riots were. It's only in retrospect that they've been given status as the launching moment of the gay liberation movement.

And the publication of *Maurice* was part of that?

In a sense, it was a part of that revolution—a gay novel launched into a still generally hostile world. The straight press, that is to say the mainstream establishment media, was not prepared to acknowledge the possibility of a forthright gay relationship ending happily. One reviewer dismissed *Maurice* as "ill-written, humourless, and deeply embarrassing," and another review was entitled "Fairy Tale."

Oh, that is cruel.

But you can wear those attacks as a badge of honour. *Maurice*, even coming out 50 years after you had written it, was still ahead of its time.

I see, I guess. So it was pilloried by heterosexuals and welcomed by homosexuals?

Reaction amongst homosexuals was a bit more complex than that. Some who were involved in gay liberation saw the storyline as too romanticized, particularly the ending, when Alec and I head off to live in peace and tranquility. These gay critics were disappointed that the characters were not depicted as taking up the human rights struggle.

But there wasn't a human rights struggle for homosexuals in Edwardian England.

You're right. And so that critique did somewhat miss the point of how revolutionary *Maurice* was. Is.

Indeed.

Of far greater impact is the fact that reading *Maurice* has been hugely significant for countless numbers of gay people in their own coming-out process. They've drawn inspiration from it. In the story of Alec and me finding each other, falling in love, and living our lives together, they have found hope that such a life and such a future may be possible for them as well.

Really?

Really.

My, my. I guess that is a rather nice legacy that I have left. I'm rather humbled.

And, my dear friend and creator, I get to live that legacy every time a gay person picks up and reads *Maurice*. And for that, I'm eternally grateful.

Now, don't get maudlin on me.

Ha-ha. Don't worry, Morgan. You're not getting off that easily. I'll forever chastise you for not releasing me out into the world decades earlier.

So be it.

———

References

Forster, E. M. *Maurice*. Harmondsworth, Middlesex: Edward Arnold, 1971.

———. *A Room with a View*. Harmondsworth, Middlesex: Edward Arnold, 1908.

Furbank, P. N. *E. M. Forster, A Life*. 2 vols. Oxford: Oxford University Press, 1979.

Galgut, Damon. *Arctic Summer—A Novel*. Toronto: McClelland & Stewart, 2014.

Gorton, Don. "While *Maurice* Slept," *The Gay and Lesbian Review*, XXI, 6 (November–December 2014).

LaFontaine, David. "Forster without *Maurice* (still gay)," *The Gay and Lesbian Review*, XXI, 5 (September–October 2014).

Moffatt, Wendy. *A Great Unrecorded History, A New Life of E. M. Forster*. New York: Farrar, Straus, and Giroux, 2010.

about time

"I HAVE TO GO, MOM. NEED TO GET BACK TO studying. Give Dad my best." Grant put the receiver down, perhaps a little too quickly. He hoped she hadn't noticed.

He got up from his desk and dove onto the bed. He picked up the book from the nightstand.

Grant frowned at the slight tear on the cover. The rip obscured a bit of the illustration, but not enough to interfere with the predictable quickening of his heart as he stared at the drawing—golden-haired Billy sitting on a bench, one running shoe in his hands as he's glancing at his coach Harlan, who is standing slightly behind him, his hands clutching a towel around his waist, his muscular pecs, thighs, and calves clearly visible. Just over Harlan's head is the wording, "By Patricia Nell Warren." A black sliver ran the width of the cover above her name, and then came the title, *The Front Runner*, in large black lettering. Grant liked the boldness of the font. Centred above the title was the marketing squib, "The controversial coast-to-coast bestseller—an unusual love story, as moving as any ever written." At the very top in tiny script was a rooster logo, a few asterisks, "$1.75," and "A Bantam Book."

The novel was first published in 1974. Grant's 1975 copy was already from the fifth printing. All his friends were reading it. Well, those of his friends who were readers were reading it—and enough other people to make it the first gay book on the *New York*

Times best-seller list. That's what had initially attracted Grant to it. Something historic was going on here, socially and politically. But once he got into the story, he found that it became much more personal. The sex scenes made for great jerking-off material, a benefit to reading it at night in bed. But it was also giving him dreams—night dreams and daydreams—that had to do with things much bigger than sex. Something major was going on for him personally as he read it.

———

Athletes had been an obsession from when he was 6 or 7 years old, still in primary school, not as in watching games on the playing field or on TV, but rather close up and in his fantasies.

Grant's most frequent proximity to athletes was on the trolley bus as he rode to his weekly music lesson or to get his monthly allergy shot. Pretending to be engrossed in a book, he would steal glances across the aisle at the university guys heading to or from class. His preference was for those wearing a football jacket, WLU Golden Hawks or U of W Warriors. If they were alone, they'd be sitting staring out the window. Invariably, they'd have their knees spread wide apart or one foot propped up on the seat or legs stretched out into the aisle. They never sat with their legs crossed. On noticing, Grant always uncrossed his. If there were a group of them together, they'd be talking loudly, laughing, punching each other in the shoulder, and tossing crumpled coffee cups or empty Coke cans at each other, which, if they happened to roll under a seat, would be ignored and left there.

But it wasn't only the football jocks that caught his attention. Grant didn't know the term *jocks* in those days. He'd only heard it once he got into high school. And then he relished it. Most of the university guys on the bus would interest him as long as they weren't homely-looking. Homely was what Grant thought of himself. A gym bag on a guy's lap or at his feet was as much of a trigger as a football jacket, particularly if it were open enough for Grant to glimpse a rumpled T-shirt, or gym shorts or running shoes or dirty socks, or other gear that he couldn't identify but which he longed to examine more closely.

They never seemed to notice him. That was okay with Grant, because then he could furtively look at them. The possibility that one of them might speak to him had crossed his mind, and that prospect filled him with terror. But he'd come up with a strategy. Grant had perfected what he thought was a convincing imitation of a deaf mute by watching Trevor down the street. He never had to draw on this strategy. Such absence of cause both relieved and disappointed him.

Grant thought it pathetic that he placed so much stock in his bus rides. But it was the closest that he could get. To what, he had no words to describe. It was a feeling, dark and compelling. He sensed it was illicit and never breathed a word about it to anyone.

———

Each night with *The Front Runner* in bed, Grant would open the book at the beginning and skim through what he had read previously. He wouldn't reread it—just look for those sentences and paragraphs that he had highlighted. The yellow marker was a constant companion, though it carried risks. More than once, it had slipped off his lap and left a mark on the sheets. He paused now over the last highlighted sentence:

> It was in 1962, that first year of coaching at Villanova, that I had finally had to confess to myself that my feelings had a name: homosexuality.

Harlan would have been 27 by then. Grant's rush of self-righteousness made him smile. He had been able to name his feelings at a very much younger age, not as early as those preteen years when he was first ogling the university guys on the bus, but rather around puberty. It was shortly after the backyard camping party.

Dad had warned the boys to keep the noise down. It was a big deal for Grant to be allowed to have Bart and Steven over for a summer sleepover in the tent in the backyard, to have a party with friends free from his pestering brothers. The three of them had been giggling too loudly. Now, Grant was intent on avoiding a repeat of his father's threat to bring them inside, as halfhearted as the threat had been made. His mom had, no doubt, put him up to it.

They were the same age, their birthdays within a few months of each other, and were in the same Grade 5 class at school. But Bart might as well have been in high school. He always knew more, had done more. At least that's what he said, convincingly. Now in the hushed dimness of their flashlights, he proposed that they play strip poker. Grant jumped at the idea. Steven always went along with whatever Bart or Grant suggested. So strip poker it was, except that only Bart knew how to play poker. They settled on strip crazy eights. It didn't take many rounds before they were all naked. Grant loved the excitement and was disappointed that it appeared they'd come to a dead end. What was left to do? Bart, with uncharacteristic hesitancy, said, "Well, we could milk each other." Steven looked perplexed but said nothing. Grant dismissed the idea out of hand. "Boys don't give off milk from their tits, stupid." At that moment, for once, he felt superior to Bart. For years after, he rued his naivety. What a lost opportunity.

It wasn't much later when Grant discovered what Bart had meant.

He could remember where it was and when it was: in the showers after gym class. He regularly got aroused and would go to great lengths to hide it. He just knew, somehow, that he mustn't let on. It was embarrassing and confusing, because the other boys didn't seem to have the same problem. There'd be the usual horseplay in the showers and locker room, and the snapping of wet towels on each other's behinds. But his classmates didn't take any great pains to cover their nakedness unless they were among the unfortunate ones with small dicks who would be subjected to endless ribbing. None of the other kids got erections like he did, at least not that he could see. Then one day, it happened. He was taking his time drying off so the other boys would all leave and wouldn't see him naked. This time, he kept rubbing the towel on his penis. The sensation felt so wonderful, more than wonderful. He kept it up until, with a giant shudder roiling up and down his body, there was suddenly sticky white stuff coming out of his dick. It sure wasn't pee. It didn't look like pee, and he had never felt this way when he had peed. His first thought was one of horror: *I've broken myself.* Then just as instantly, he understood. It wasn't just that he liked looking at the other guys; it was that he really, really, really liked looking at them. And his cock had responded.

He didn't have a word for it, but he now knew that he liked boys "in that way" and not girls "in that way." It was a relief to know what was going on, but it was also frustrating, because he couldn't do anything about it except in private. His initial towelling system led to ever more inventive strategies for masturbating. But it took years, painstakingly long years, before the fantasized physical contact with another guy became reality.

At 18, he had three part-time jobs: shovelling snow in the winter and mowing lawns in the summer around his neighbourhood, packing groceries at Zehr's market, and performing his paper route. He was the oldest newspaper delivery boy that he knew of in town. But it was decent money, and he had stuff he wanted to buy, books mainly.

One Saturday morning, Grant knocked on the apartment door of a new customer on his route. There was no answer, so he knocked again. He heard shuffling noises from inside and then the sound of a deadbolt being unlocked. The door opened, and a tall grey-haired man sporting a large scruffy moustache stood staring at Grant, a burgundy housecoat belted around his waist. "Collecting for *The Record*, sir," Grant said.

"Ah, yeah, of course, come in," the man replied. Grant stepped inside. The Saturday-morning sunlight shining in through the windows at the back of the apartment barely reached the front living room. As Grant's eyes adjusted to the dimness, he saw two overstuffed chairs grouped on each side of a stained coffee table. A floor lamp with a fringed shade cast pale light onto the chairs. Newspapers and magazines and empty beer bottles sat on the small Arborite dining table against the opposite wall.

"I'll be right back. I'll get the money," the man said. He headed down the apartment hallway, turning right into the bedroom. "Oh, how much is it?"

"A dollar eighty-five. For the week."

"Okay."

Grant fiddled with his punch and the new subscriber's card that he had prepared. The smell of cigarette smoke and stale beer was a touch intoxicating, a slightly exotic world so different from his home environment.

He looked up as his customer came back into the living room. His mouth dropped. No longer secured around his waist, the dressing gown hung open, revealing a hairy chest and a big cock dangling down. His customer chuckled and headed over to one of the large stuffed chairs. He placed the change on the side table and then dropped into the chair, his dressing gown draped along the side of his body, his legs spread wide apart. "Come over here, son," he said quietly, beckoning Grant with his fingers.

Grant didn't hesitate. He walked right over and stood in front of him, glancing occasionally at his face but mostly continuing to gawk at the man's penis. "Come a little closer." Grant stepped closer. The man sat more upright and reached up, slipping his hand into Grant's belt. The punch and subscriber card dropped to the floor. "Let's see what we have here," the man said as he began to unbuckle Grant's belt. He loosened it and then slid the zipper open, manoeuvring Grant's pants down to his ankles. He cupped his hand on the growing bulge in Grant's underpants. Grant almost swooned. The man turned his head up, and Grant looked into his eyes. "Do you like this?" he asked softly as he gently massaged Grant's crotch.

"Um ... um ... yes, sir ... yes ... yes, I do."

The man lowered his head and in one quick movement pulled Grant's underpants down, lifted Grant's penis and balls up, and slipped the boy's genitals into his mouth. The warmth of the man's mouth on his cock sent Grant off balance; he had to grab onto the man's head to avoid toppling over. He was slightly conscious of the man moving his tongue around his penis and drawing it in and out of his mouth, pressing his lips against the head each time. Grant's heart was pounding. The moist heat of the man's mouth intensified. Grant held on more firmly to the man's head, letting his hands move in tandem with the man's back-and-forth movement on his cock.

Grant's whole body started to gyrate. His legs became so wobbly that he had to lean over so that he was resting his chest right on top of the man's head. And the man, holding firmly onto Grant's rigid penis, kept moving it in and out of his mouth with increasing rapidity. Grant exploded, over and over and over, spasms whipping through his body. Grant locked his arms around the man's head and shoulders, resting his full body weight on him. His legs were useless. The man kept Grant's penis in his mouth but dropped his hands and wrapped his arms around Grant's body. He held him tightly, Grant panting. Neither of them moved for what seemed a long time. Eventually, Grant felt strength return to his legs. He placed his body's weight back on his legs and straightened himself up. The man took hold of Grant's penis once more as he slipped it out of his mouth and smiled as he watched it flinching in his palm. Grant looked down at it too and smiled for a moment. He then stepped back, almost tripping with his underwear and pants still wrapped around his ankles, and began hooting and hollering and pumping his fists up into the air above his head.

For the next year or so, Grant looked forward with great anticipation to the Saturday-morning collection time. He was never disappointed.

———⌣———

Grant realized that he was reading one of the first gay sex scenes he had ever seen in a book.

> I went to my knees, sliding down against him and kissing his body all the way down. My hands shucked down his shorts and jockstrap both at once. The harsh brown patch of pubic hair was startling on his pale, supple, veined loins, and the swollen cock between those runner's thighs. I had it in my mouth almost before I'd seen it. The only sound, in that silence, was Billy groaning softly as he fondled my head and thrust his hips slowly against my face.

He read the paragraph again and then a third time.

Art imitating life. It was not too much of a stretch to transpose his own first time with this scene of the initial sex between Harlan and Billy in *The Front Runner*. Well, it was a bit of a stretch. His scrawny 18-year-old body was hardly the taut muscled frame of a university marathon runner like Billy Sive, and his paper route customer's body was a far cry from the chiselled Harlan Brown. But so what—a little reverse artistic license. The setup was the same: the older man fondling the younger one, taking his cock into his mouth, fingering and pulling on his balls, a rocking back and forth building to an explosive climax.

Grant was so grateful to his newspaper customer for

introducing him to this world of wonders. He could look forward to getting sucked off every Saturday morning. He was aware, not knowing how but feeling it instinctively, that this all must be kept private. Sure, his customer had said that first time, "Now, this will be our little secret, you understand?" But the admonition didn't carry nearly as much force as some awareness deep in his gut that this was something that no one, most of all his parents, must find out about, not just the Saturday-morning blowjobs but also his attraction to the other boys' bodies in the showers. And when he thought back to times on the bus when he was as young as 6 and staring above the cover of his book at the university guys in the seats across from him, even then he somehow knew that he shouldn't tell anyone.

Now here he was in his own apartment at 25 years of age with a *New York Times* best seller in his hands reading descriptions of what he had fantasized and what he experienced himself.

———

Reading *The Front Runner* each evening was bringing back a flood of memories for Grant.

> I was dating a girl named Mary Ellen Bache ... I managed to get her in trouble. Of course, it was my duty to marry her, and I did.

In the backstory to *The Front Runner*, Harlan had a child before he came to terms with his sexual orientation, before he met and fell in love with Billy. Grant wondered whether somewhere out there in the wide world, he had a child too.

Grant had had sex with women. Well, one woman. But multiple times with her.

He almost had had sex with a woman one Saturday morning with his newspaper customer. His customer, arriving at the door totally nude, as had become his routine when he heard Grant's knock, took Grant's hand and led him into the bedroom. "Grant, I want you to meet Sylvia." An attractive woman, younger than his newspaper customer, lay in bed smiling up at him, the sheets pulled down enough to expose her breasts.

She patted the bed and said, "Glad to meet you, Grant. I've heard a lot about you. Come on … sit down here beside me."

Grant was petrified and resentful.

The Saturday-morning suck jobs by his newspaper customer had become an exhilarating orgasmic routine that Grant looked forward to all week long. He had on occasion fondled the older man's large penis. Grant asked him once if cum would come out of his cock too if he, Grant, put it in his mouth. The man chuckled and said, "That would take a long time." Grant was disappointed with the casualness with which his suggestion had been brushed off. He had wanted to ramp up the experimentation but didn't feel confident enough to press the issue.

Over these many Saturday-morning visits, it had only been Grant and the older man—a secret, intimate, comfortable relationship. Now, there was someone else who had come into this world—and a woman at that.

Grant looked back and forth between Sylvia and his newspaper customer.

The man laid his hand on Grant's shoulder and asked, "Would you like to join us, Sylvia and me?" There was no pressure or insistence in his voice, just an open invitation. This wasn't the kind of ramping up of experimentation that appealed to Grant. He gruffly excused himself and left without having collected the newspaper money. He slammed the door on his way out.

The man moved out of his apartment the following week. He didn't cancel his newspaper subscription. He just disappeared. Grant was disappointed and blamed himself.

Two years later, Grant had a summer job that had him driving around Ontario in his first car—an old VW Beetle. He landed in

Ottawa for a gathering of the other 10 young people contracted by the government to visit and assess summer youth employment projects.

There was an immediate easy camaraderie within the group at the initial session. They had great summer jobs with responsibility, authority, and a travel budget. What was not to like? Sandra sat across the table from him. Grant couldn't help noticing her breasts. They were large and, as far as he could tell, unshackled by a bra. It was, after all, the late 1960s. Grant noticed that Sandra noticed that Grant had noticed. She slid down in her chair so that her blouse pulled tighter against her chest, and she smiled an open, mischievous smile. Grant blushed and looked down at his papers.

In the meeting, Sandra rarely spoke, but when she did, it was always to say something smart and insightful. Grant admired that. He was prone to be too talkative and often regretted his prosaic comments the moment they were out of his mouth. At dinner that evening, Sandra sat next to him. Their knees touched. He flinched but didn't draw away. She pressed her knee harder against his. He had an instant hard-on. That shocked him. He had never been aroused by a girl or a woman before. She deftly and inconspicuously slid her hand onto his thigh, placed it on his crotch, and squeezed. He came instantly. The boisterous chatter around the table masked his gasps. No one noticed.

He spent the night in her bed, and they made love over and over again. Grant was thrilled.

Grant saw Sandra again at the end-of-summer wrap-up session of the group. She greeted him with a friendly peck on his cheek. He waited for an invitation to her bed. None came. He was surprised but not particularly upset. Over the course of the summer, as he travelled around in his VW, he'd had sex with four guys—great sex.

Sandra of the summer project was the one and only woman with whom he had had sex. But he had wondered over the years since then if there were a little Sandra or a little Grant somewhere in the world. If so, it apparently hadn't been a case like Harlan's, of him getting Sandra "in trouble" with an expectation on Sandra's part that it was his "duty to marry her." Maybe she just wanted sex. Or maybe she just wanted a baby. It was the '60s, after all.

———— ❦ ————

Grant underlined another couple of sentences, turned down the corner of the page, and closed the book.

> Spending an entire night together was such a luxury. We went to sleep pressed tightly together, lying on our sides. Billy fitted into the curve of my body, his back against my chest, my arms around him.

Grant thought of his first night cuddling with Curtis after sex. It was such a luxury, unlike the usual sex on the run he'd been having.

Grant had been excited about the party at Maureen's parents' farm with friends celebrating the end of freshman year. There would be music, beer, and pot. And definitely there would be sex—amongst some of them. Maureen and studly Jasper were known to be doing it all the time in Jasper's dorm room. The weekend party would afford the chance for other couplings. But Grant didn't know of any other guys going who shared his interest in male-on-male coupling. He hadn't come out to any in their close-knit group. Indeed, in conversations through the school year, he had embellished last summer's connection to Sandra into a months-long torrid affair. He was setting himself up for a disappointing weekend at the farm. How disappointing was clear to him by Saturday morning, when he awoke stiff from sleeping on the cold ground, badly hung over and horned up from a night of imaging himself in Maureen's place in the double sleeping bag with Jasper.

He faked a cold, excused himself from the party, got into his VW Beetle, and headed not back home to Waterloo but rather to Toronto.

Clandestine weekend trips were becoming his thing. This was the third one in the past few months. He had treated himself to an extended Easter weekend, catching a cheap last-minute deal to San Juan, Puerto Rico. His parents didn't feel that they could object: he had racked up stellar grades during the year and was paying for the trip himself. The first night in San Juan, Grant fell head over heels for a hot Latino med student he picked up in a gay bar after a Shirley Bassey concert. Raul was the most beautiful man he had ever had sex with. The sex wasn't great, but so what? Raul was a knockout. Grant was so enamoured that he returned to San Juan for the long Victoria Day weekend in May, but this trip cost him a lot more. He was so anxious to go that he bought a ticket at regular fare, not wanting to risk his chances if no cheap last-minute deals were available. He told his parents that he was going to a friend's cottage in Muskoka. When Grant arrived in San Juan, Raul told him that he was unavailable, that he had exams that he had to study for all weekend. But his half brother was free. Luis was not as good-looking as Raul. He was shorter, was black, and was a far better lover than Raul. On the previous trip, Grant had enjoyed being seen out in public with Raul. On this trip, Grant enjoyed having sex all weekend long with Luis.

Now, after this party at Maureen's parents' farm, Grant headed off toward Toronto again, but he drove past the airport this time and into the city centre. He was frustrated when the YMCA on Grosvenor Street had no rooms available. That was the cheapest place to stay, but equally important was that it was the easiest place to find sex. He had discovered the propped-open-bedroom-door-cruising lifestyle on the residence floors last year and had availed himself of many of the Y's amenities over the course of the winter. With the Y not an option, he booked himself into a grungy guest house next door and slept for most of the day.

Around ten o'clock, he showered and got dressed and headed out for a night on the town. The St. Charles Tavern was right around the corner on Yonge Street. Grant sat himself on a stool at the big horseshoe-shaped bar, ordered a draft, and eyed the sparse crowd around the room. It was still early for a Saturday night.

Grant was halfway through his first draft when a pair of arms wrapped around him from behind. The hug was powerful and erotic. A head leaned in and whispered in his ear, "I must have you." Grant almost laughed, but he didn't. He placed his hands on the muscular forearms hugging his torso and gave them a receptive squeeze. He swivelled around on his stool and came face-to-face, Grant's white face to Curtis's black face. They asked each other questions and responded. Grant: student from out of town; in Toronto for the weekend; here alone; staying in a guest house around the corner; no boyfriend. Curtis: a recently retired ballet dancer; lives alone in an apartment nearby; here alone; no boyfriend.

Curtis insisted that Grant check out of the guest house and stay with him at his place. Grant did, spending the entire night with Curtis. And he did the same a few weeks later—and about one weekend a month for the next year and a half. Grant told his parents that he was using the research facilities at the University of Toronto Library and staying with a friend. They didn't press him for details.

Grant moved in with Curtis, sort of. They lived together, sort of. After sex, they would sleep pressed tightly together, lying on their sides, Grant fitted into the curve of Curtis's body, his back against Curtis's chest, Curtis's arms wrapped around him. The last thing Curtis would say each night, whispering in his ear, was "I've got you. I love you, Babe. And I've got you."

Grant was envious of Harlan and Billy. Sure, they were facing hostility and discrimination in the track and field world as Billy won more and more races nationally and internationally. The suspicions about his sexual orientation were bad enough for the homophobic members of the athletic establishment, but the escalating rumours that he was in a sexual relationship with his coach, well, that made the sports hierarchy apoplectic and fired the media into a frenzy. But at least Harlan and Billy had each other, a real loving relationship of which the sexual component was only one part. They were living together full time in Harlan's house on campus. They were a couple.

Grant rolled his eyes. How could he be envious of two fictional characters in a novel? He knew people had imagined themselves in the storylines of classic novels for centuries, coveting the dramatic romantic lives of the characters. He had read his fair share. But those characters had always been straight—or almost always. He was aware of earlier gay books, like James Baldwin's *Giovanni's Room* and Gore Vidal's *The Pillar and the City*. But *The Front Runner* was different. For one thing, it was a contemporary novel—Billy was hoping to compete at the 1976 Montreal Summer Olympics. And it was more than that. Reading *The Front Runner* was giving Grant a vision of what might be possible for him, something more than just sex, something he hadn't had yet, something he knew he wanted.

He certainly didn't have it with Curtis. For the first six months or so, he thought maybe he did. The sex was great for the most part. Well, maybe not so great. It was always the same. They would go to bed, and Curtis would fuck him and then give him a compensatory blowjob. There was some romance. Grant liked the Sunday morning brunches out in restaurants, like a real couple. But after about six months, the novelty wore off. Grant decided it was better that they not see each other so much. Then the real drama set in: gay melodrama, crying scenes, pleading scenes, Curtis promising the moon if Grant would only stay. And Grant would give in. Then the cycle would start over again. Causing someone so much evident pain made Grant feel terrible, but he didn't love Curtis. He knew that. After another year of Curtis's histrionics, Grant had had enough. He left and never came back.

Grant was the one to do the leaving in his second relationship, too, his affair with Antonio. But it was so different. It wasn't because he didn't love Antonio; it was because he loved Antonio so much.

They met one night at the Quest, a small upstairs gay dance bar diagonally across the corner from the apartment building where Grant was now living in downtown Toronto. It was October 1974. He had finished one graduate degree in Waterloo and had started another at the University of Toronto. In an exception to his general rule not to party on weeknights, he and friends were at the Quest celebrating someone or other's birthday. He noticed a man watching him from the far side of the bar—about 10 years older than he and very handsome, distinguished. Grant smiled back, and the man immediately walked over and introduced himself. Grant liked such self-confidence. It reminded him of Sandra.

They started chatting, but the music and boisterousness of Grant's partying friends made that difficult. Antonio took Grant's hand and led him to a far corner that was quieter. Grant learned in short order that Antonio was different from most Quest patrons. He was a well-established businessman. With neither pretension nor false modesty, Antonio told him his last name and watched Grant's face as the name recognition of the large family-owned business struck home. With similar candour, Antonio told Grant that he was married. He had an agreement with his wife that he was free to go out to gay bars, or wherever, one night a week. Before the night was over, he would drive home to the bed he shared with his wife and the home in which they were raising their children. He would tell Stephanie everything that had happened. They were totally open with each other. Stephanie was okay with Antonio spending that time in his gay world because he had committed to never leave her or the family. And apparently, as far as Grant could tell, it was a commitment made wholeheartedly out of love for her and the children, not a compromise resentfully agreed to.

Grant was smitten. He wasn't bothered about the bisexual thing. Quite the reverse.

He took hold of Antonio's hand and led him out of the Quest and across the street to his apartment. They made love. At two in the morning, Antonio got up out of Grant's bed, showered, kissed Grant good night, and went home to his wife. Grant and Antonio spent the next Tuesday night, or rather part of it, together—and the Tuesday night after that. This happened week after week.

Before long, Grant was far beyond smitten. He had fallen in love. He would tell Antonio that he loved him. Antonio would reply that he knew. Antonio never told Grant that he loved him. Grant knew that he did.

In December, Grant decided to throw a Christmas party in his small studio apartment. He thought that it would be fun to crowd as many friends into it as he could. The more, the merrier. He decorated his place with Christmas ornaments scrounged from the attic in his parents' home. They were pleased that he had an interest in these trappings from family Christmases past. He invited fellow graduate students from U of T, gay friends who were part of the regular Quest clan, and Antonio and Stephanie.

It was the first time that he had met Stephanie, and he found her absolutely charming. She was gorgeous. That was no surprise, since Antonio was so handsome. They made a stunning-looking couple. Stephanie was gregarious and totally at ease with the young crowd squeezed into Grant's apartment, most of them gay men.

The party was a great success.

Grant's friends, at least the closer ones who knew that he and Antonio were lovers, had mixed reactions about Grant's having invited Stephanie. During party postmortems over the following few days, some of them expressed awe at how everyone—meaning Grant, Antonio, and Stephanie—got along so well together. A few expressed skepticism. Their critiques were well meant. They were concerned about Grant getting hurt. Grant reassured them that it was all cool.

His friends weren't so tactless as to sing "Smoke Gets in Your Eyes."

Tuesdays with Antonio were great; the other six days without him, not so much. Grant found himself getting nostalgic for the weekend brunch excursions that he had had with Curtis. The loneliness was complicated. He missed Antonio—the company and the sex. He had a robust social circle, so he could fill some of his free time by going out with friends. But he didn't feel right about sleeping with other guys. More accurately, he didn't feel like it. Antonio had insisted that they not expect monogamy of each other. Without it having to be said, they both recognized the hypocrisy such an expectation would have represented given his agreement with Stephanie. Grant was quite sure that Antonio's adamant stand was for Grant's sake. Antonio only had one night for his gay life and he was spending that with Grant, so it was pretty clear that Antonio was not sleeping with other guys. But he was getting sex, with his wife, the other nights. Grant, on the other hand, had no such option and yet had a city full of options. He just didn't feel like acting on them, at least not often.

The last thing Grant wanted to be was the nagging mistress. He said nothing about his frustration, and tried not to let it be apparent in nonverbal ways either. Against his will, he thought about Antonio and his life with Stephanie a lot. Knowing that they had a Toronto Symphony Orchestra subscription, Grant bought a ticket one night in March for the same performance that Antonio and Stephanie were going to. He got there early and hung around in the lobby, watching as the audience arrived. About 15 minutes before the concert began, he saw them come in and head toward their orchestra seats. Grant could see them from where he was sitting in the balcony. For much of the first half, they were either holding hands or Antonio had his arm around Stephanie's shoulders. To all appearances, they were a loving couple in a secure, well-adjusted marriage. To Grant's regret, he knew that to be the truth.

Grant left at intermission.

The next Tuesday, Grant told Antonio that that would be their last night together. Antonio was quiet and then said simply, "I understand." Grant had hoped for some Curtis-like protest. They made love in silence, after which Antonio got dressed and left—without showering.

Grant cried for three days.

Grant let the book flip closed, his finger lodged inside to keep his place. Billy's last comment had jarred him.

> "So you weren't open about being gay in school," I said.

> "No. I wasn't," Billy replied. "I kept very quiet about it. I didn't feel guilty or anything. But I felt very intimidated by straight attitudes, the more I learned about them. I'm not really a brave person, maybe. But when I felt troubled, I could always go and talk it out with my dad."

Grant thought back to the weekend after his breakup with Antonio. He had kept to his usual schedule and visited his parents. He was subdued and they had noticed. They asked if something was wrong. He told them that he was under a lot of stress in his graduate program. They seemed skeptical. Grant, claiming that he had a ton of reading to do and essays to write, left early to return to his apartment.

He took another sip of beer and set the can back down on

the nightstand. He looked out the window and down toward the street, watching the rain reflecting off the lights of the cars. His reading chair, a fancy designation for the comfy armchair that he had picked up at Goodwill, was positioned against the window so he could enjoy the view.

Arranging furniture in his small studio apartment had been a challenge. The best feature of the place was the large window that spanned the 12-foot width of the apartment and went from the ceiling to within 10 inches of the floor. In addition to his reading chair and the nightstand, he had the head of his bed crammed up against the window so that he could look down on the street life last thing at night and first thing in the morning and when he was fucking a guy in his bed. He had drapes but usually left them open. His exhibitionist streak got off on the idea that the whole world could see whatever hot guy he was topping that night. It was more erotic concept than reality since his apartment was on the twenty-sixth floor and no one from street level could see up into it. Maybe someone from one of the nearby buildings could, but those were mainly office towers that were vacant at night. He kept the drapes closed during the time that he was seeing Antonio, less out of discretion than intimacy.

The drapes were kept open the night he brought Tim home.

The McDonald's where he met Tim was on Yonge Street, less than a block from his apartment building. Grant had a circuit for his evening meals: one night at KFC, the next night at Burger King, the third night at McDonald's. Repeat. For some reason, he had never picked up the talent of cooking when he was growing up at home. His mom had taught him how to iron a shirt. That was a really useful skill.

It was a McDonald's night, shortly after the breakup with Antonio, when his friend Jason dropped in and squeezed into the booth with him. Jason started chattering away about how it was all for the best and he had tried to warn him earlier that it wouldn't, couldn't, end well with Antonio. Yadditty, yadditty, yadditty. Grant wasn't paying much attention, partly because he didn't want to talk about it, but mainly because he couldn't take his eyes off the hunk that Jason had with him. He was the hottest-looking man that Grant has seen since ... well, probably since Raul. The guy was meeting Grant's gaze and smiling back. Jason paused in his rambling when he finally noticed that the other two were staring at each other and ignoring him. Jason sighed and introduced Grant to Tim and Tim to Grant. Tim, it turned out, was a cousin of Jason's who had recently moved to Toronto from a small town in northern Ontario.

Grant reached across the table and shook Tim's hand. "Nice to meet you. Welcome to Toronto."

Grant went to release his grip, but Tim held on. Tim raised his other hand and brushed it back and forth along Grant's forearm. "I really like a guy with hairy arms. I think it's so hot."

That was it. Grant left his Big Mac and fries half eaten. He had Tim in his apartment in no time. Tim, still enthralled with the big city, loved the view from Grant's bed.

They started dating, like, real dating—going out to movies and restaurants, dancing at the clubs on weekends, and sleeping together. That last always happened at Grant's place. Tim was living in a two-bedroom apartment in the sprawling housing complex St. James Town. He had three roommates, young women whom he had known in his hometown up north. All four of them had come to Toronto at the same time to find jobs and husbands.

On the first warm weekend in May, Grant took Tim to Hanlan's Point on Toronto Islands, the gay beach, the clothing-optional gay beach. Tim was stripped in a second. Grant, the more modest of the two, kept his bathing suit on. All day, friends and mere acquaintances of Grant would amble by and, on some pretense or another, stop for a conversation. Being new in town, Tim was a fresh face for the gay crowd. As rugged as his facial features were, that was not the part of his body that they focused on. Tim was well-muscled, everywhere. He relished the attention almost as much as Grant was relishing showing him off.

A day by the water was also in the cards for early July, but that was a world away. Grant's parents had a trailer in a park up in Haliburton cottage country. Months ago, he had promised that he would come up for a visit. But now he had a boyfriend. He had never introduced his parents to any of his gay friends. They had never discussed his social life, not since his dating of girls in high school had petered out. His parents didn't ask questions. Grant didn't offer information.

Grant called his parents and asked them if it would be okay if he brought a friend along up to the trailer. They would drive up on Sunday, spend the day with them, and then stay over at the trailer for a couple of days after his parents returned to Waterloo for the workweek. The arrangements were fine with his folks.

The day went well. Tim, having grown up in northern Ontario, was delighted for the chance to get out fishing on a beautiful summer day. Grant, Grant's dad, and Tim spent the better part of the afternoon in the boat. Grant's father managed a body shop in Waterloo, and Tim had a passion for disassembling and rebuilding car engines. The two of them talked nonstop for most of the time, interrupted only by the excitement of the occasional landing of a fish, mainly small bass. They'd throw them back in.

Amish Lake was not known for being a particularly good fishing lake, so Grant's mom hadn't counted on the men providing the supplies for supper. Hamburgers were the order of the day, perfect in Grant's mind as a camping dinner.

As the meal wore down and his parents began organizing themselves to head home, his mother trained her eye steadily on Grant and said casually, "And you remember, Grant, if the two of you want to sleep together, the table at the far end of the trailer folds down into a double bed. There are clean sheets already on the mattress. The pillows are in the cupboard overhead."

Grant blanched. Tim fiddled with the remaining crumbs of his third hamburger on his empty plate. Grant's father paused for a moment, looked back and forth at the other three, and then continued packing the car.

"Okay, thanks, Mom," Grant mumbled. "Dad, I presume you want us to haul the boat up out of the water before we leave?"

"That's right. Chain it up to the tree. Put the fuel tank in the shed. Just make sure you lock the shed and hide the key underneath the trailer where I showed you earlier."

"Okay."

That was it—the most significant non-conversation with his parents about his sexual orientation in all of his 24 years.

It was also one of the last dates he had with Tim. Perhaps the family awkwardness played a role. Tim insisted that wasn't it. It was just that, being new to the big city, he didn't want to be tied to just one guy. He wanted to date others. Grant's translation to himself: Tim had tired of him. It wasn't a good feeling at all.

———

Grant had always been a voracious solitary reader. As a child, he devoured every one of the *Hardy Boys Mystery Series* books in the Waterloo Public Library, and then, feeling self-conscious, he moved on surreptitiously to the *Nancy Drew, Girl Detective* series. Only his librarian knew for sure. English literature had been his favourite subject in high school. He relished taking creative approaches to essay assignments. He was particularly proud of one he wrote for Miss Duncan in Grade 10 comparing the protagonists' struggles in Paul Bunyan's *Pilgrim's Progress* and James Joyce's *Portrait of an Artist as a Young Man*. Though excited about what he was reading and writing, he didn't talk about it at the supper table at home. Neither of his parents, children of the Depression, had had the chance to finish high school. Grant loved them and didn't want to come off as sounding pretentious. His older brother was too busy with girls to care, and his younger brother was already intimidated by him.

He took a year off during his undergraduate studies to go to Paris, spending a lonely monastic but intellectually stimulating winter in the libraries of the Sorbonne reading widely on subjects that didn't fit into the curriculum of his psychology courses in Waterloo.

But in all of his years of reading at home and in Paris and since moving to Toronto, he had rarely been gripped by a book like he was by *The Front Runner*. Sure, it was a well-written dramatic story and he was stirred by the eroticism, but it had become a personal and a political read in a way that was unique in Grant's experience. The story was about Billy and Harlan, but it felt like it was about him too.

———

Billy had qualified to be part of the American track and field team for the Montreal Olympics. The hostility against him because he was gay was increasing in tandem with his rising visibility. The implied and explicit threats were multiplying. He and Harlan tried to keep the static from interfering with his training. Finding the time and the opportunity to be together as a couple was a struggle and a risk.

The stress in reading the descriptions of the qualifying heats and then the final races was such that Grant slowed his pace down to a crawl. He read each paragraph twice. When Billy won the gold medal in a record-breaking 27:28:9 in the 10,000-metre, Grant actually shouted out loud.

The crucial 5,000-metre final was coming up in a few days.

> "I'm going to come out of the Athletes Village tonight," he said, "and we'll spend the night together. I really need you." The bodyguards brought Billy to the hotel, and we all searched the room for bombs, and then the bodyguards left and camped in the corridor outside. We locked the door, and were alone for the first time in a week.

Grant glanced down at the clock on the nightstand. He saw that the time was 1:05 a.m. His gaze lifted from the clock and swept across the bed, the empty bed.

He reopened the book and continued reading slowly, now rereading each sentence twice or three times before moving on. He did, and he did not, want to know how the story would end.

On page 275, the book shot out of Grant's hands, flying across the bed, bouncing off the bookshelf, and settling on the floor halfway down the room.

Grant gripped the arms of the chair, his heart pounding, his eyes moistening, his jaw taut.

He didn't move for ten minutes.

Then, he went over and picked up *The Front Runner*, returned to his armchair, and quietly finished the book. He placed it in his lap and looked out the window onto the deserted street below. And he made a decision.

Grant sat down at his desk, picked up a pad of paper, and selected his favourite pen.

Dear Mom and Dad,

I should have written this letter long ago. It's about time ...

He mailed the letter in the morning.

Several days later, he drove to Waterloo and spent the weekend with his parents. And they talked. They had the conversation.

And life went on. Better.

Reference

Warren, Patricia Nell. *The Front Runner*. New York: William Morrow & Company, 1974.

la bibliothèque sainte-geneviève

PETER LOOKED UP AND SMILED AT JEAN-FRANÇOIS as the latter placed the espresso on his table. The waiter frowned, not at Peter but at the tabletop. He lifted the cup and saucer and yanked a napkin from the waistband of his apron. In two rapid swirls, Jean-François dried the marble surface of the raindrops that had speckled it. He set the coffee down. Peter stared at the black hair on the back of Jean-François's wrist caught under the leather watchband. Jean-François swept his eyes over the top of Peter's head, scanning the other mostly vacant tables before pivoting and walking away, a worn copy of Camus's *L'étranger* jostling in his back pocket as he moved. He swung through the café doors and faded into the interior darkness, obscured by the etched design on the door panels and the light of the streetscape reflected on the glass—his figure just discernible propped up against the bar, his head reburied in the book.

Chilly gusts of wind swept down the street. Peter tightened his scarf. He raised the demitasse and took a sip. Lifting the saucer with his other hand, he scrutinized the table and found a tiny residue of his watery creation that Jean-François, unaware of its intent, had largely obliterated. He placed the cup amongst the droplets to reclaim what was left of his signature piece, and then balanced the saucer on top of the cup to keep the coffee warm. With his index finger, Peter traced the double gold band around the saucer's edge, coming to a halt over a barely visible finger smudge. He pressed down gently to impose his own print over the other.

He had been attracted to Café Soufflot by its proximity to the Sorbonne and la Bibliothèque Sainte-Geneviève. The style of the café's chinaware was identical to his mother's, and the interior design included walls lined with books. He imagined a tradition of French authors donating a copy of their newest book accompanied by a champagne toast as it was ceremoniously placed on a shelf.

But most of all he had made it his daily café of choice because of Jean-François.

He pulled out his pocket notebook and entered this morning's expenditure, a self-imposed meticulousness. He'd show his father that he could make it on his own.

———

Peter glanced around the Sinclair family dining room at the forces arrayed against him. His mother held his gaze for a moment before pushing her chair back, picking up the meat platter, and grumbling as she headed toward the kitchen. "I'll slice more off the roast. Offer the kids more wine, Maxwell."

His father reached awkwardly toward the buffet, teetering slightly on his chair. He grabbed the bottle of wine, topped up his own glass, and then swung the bottle around toward Peter's friends Patrick, Natalie, and Jason. "There's lots more where this comes from," his father bellowed.

"Okay," the three mumbled in unison and held out their glasses compliantly.

Peter had prepared answers about his plans for the next year that he hoped would placate these skeptics: he wanted to get a taste of Europe before settling into graduate school; there was so much he was dying to read beyond political science and economics; and he hoped to improve his French.

Madeline, his mother, had argued that the Boston libraries were perfectly adequate to meet the most esoteric of his reading interests. She was taking it personally that her son was opting to spend a year in a foreign institution rather than at the Central Library in Copley Square, to which she had devoted the better part of her career. Peter felt her position defied logic. A professional librarian should be thrilled that her son wanted to immerse himself in one of the great libraries of the Old World. During Sunday dinners, her frenetic cataloguing of the Boston Public Library's holdings in yet another microsegment of the Dewey decimal system was taxing Peter's and his father's patience. But neither of them interrupted her.

Peter's father assured his wife that he was onside, contending that if exposure to Europe was the main issue, then a couple of summer months should suffice. He'd even subsidize Peter's travel costs—but not a penny if Peter's plans extended beyond the summer. He offered to use his connections in the governor's office to get Peter useful contacts in London, Brussels, Frankfurt, and Berlin. Maybe he could even help arrange a side trip to Rome to visit the Vatican. Paris was not on the list.

Though they were relatively mute at this table, Peter's friends had been having at him for weeks now about his plans. Patrick was furious that Peter would forgo the Vietnam War protests on campus. He had been making snide remarks about Peter's commitment to the cause. Natalie was feeling abandoned. She and Peter had dated on and off since meeting during freshman year, and she had their future planned. It certainly did not include a year's separation. Jason, his roommate this past year in the dorm, generally echoed the others' objections, but with a slight threatening smirk and the occasional caustic comment about Frenchmen's "pansy propensities."

Peter's fumbling rebuttals did little to satisfy any of them. Not that it mattered. He had made up his mind.

⌣

A shrill scratching noise startled Peter awake. He shivered and pulled the musty duvet up to his neck. A movement caught his eye; he turned his head toward the narrow dormer window just in time to see a pigeon's claws slide down the slanted frost-covered pane.

He had lucked out on his first day in Paris coming across a window sign advertising this one-room garret for 250 francs a night. Fifty dollars a month for accommodation fit the tight budget that he had cobbled together from his modest savings.

Peter propped himself up against the two lumpy pillows and settled back to enjoy his new waking ritual—studying the fantasy of frost on the window, which glistened as rays of the rising sun flickered into his room. This morning he imagined a range of silvery craggy mountains interspersed with narrow crevices that cascaded down to just shy of the bottom sill. These morning window displays were something of a compensation for the newly barren nights.

Over the past week, with the sudden arrival of November night freezes, he had lost his principal community—the glittering stars visible even through the accumulated grime that coated the outside of the glass. For the previous two months since arriving, his main social interactions were nightly intimate conversations with the stars, a more engaging strategy for putting himself to sleep than counting sheep. He would recount his understanding of Kierkegaard, whom he had been reading in the library, or he would enthuse over the latest detail he had discovered in Giotto's *Saint Francis* in the Louvre. Or he would share his most recent fantasy about Jean-François.

Intent on demonstrating that not all foreign students lacked social graces, he paused from time to time to offer an opportunity for response from his friends. Mostly, the stars were content just to listen. They'd blink at him their acquiescence, and he'd carry on.

But now, the late fall frozen condensation on the single-pane glass obliterated his view of the sky from dusk to dawn. With these friends lost, his loneliness intensified.

Peter pulled one of the pillows out from behind his head and tucked it under the covers beside him. Sliding down the bed, he turned on his side and wrapped his arm around it. He closed his eyes and ran his hand slowly up and down the worn pillowcase. There were a few smooth areas. Most of it was rough to the touch, granular against his fingers. He shifted his head slightly, resting his cheek on a particularly coarse section of the fabric, and conjured up a favourite daydream.

The sound of water running through pipes in the wall signalled that his neighbour was awake. Peter threw off the duvet, slid his feet into slippers, and headed toward the door. It was best to get to the communal toilet in the hallway early. He had been an unwilling beneficiary of the olfactory gifts left behind by occupants of the other four studio apartments on his floor. Apparently, they had limited skill in perching on the raised footpads, squatting down on their haunches, and doing their business. The antiquated flushing mechanism with its calcium-encrusted faucet invariably splattered the water haphazardly, leaving much of the floor damp and sticky.

French plumbing had not made it on to the list of what he was appreciating about his year in Paris.

Washed and dressed, Peter stepped out into the hall, locked his door, and headed down the five flights. He paused on the landing before the last set of stairs and peeked over the banister. The chair propped beside the front door was empty. A set of darning needles entwined in a few centimetres of grey mohair stitching rested precariously on the edge of the seat above Mme Garneau's knitting basket. Clearly, she was up and at her concierge station this morning but must have slipped back into her apartment for a moment to answer a call of nature or to assist her enfeebled husband answer one of his.

With a bit of luck, Peter could slip out the front door. Mme Garneau had a presence that intimidated him. Part of it was physical—her heft that easily equalled two of his, the guttural baritone voice, and the left eye that never moved, not even to blink, but sat frozen in an opaque vault, leaving the right eye to compensate by darting in every direction in tandem with her animated hand gestures. About once a week, she recounted in unwavering detail the history of the childhood injury incurred when her family fled the German forces advancing on their village in the early days of the war. Recently, that story had been juxtaposed with a bemoaning of the pampered lives of contemporary young people such as her granddaughter Emilia, who was to visit any day. Mme Garneau felt that it would be good for Emilia to meet Peter. His studious nature could hopefully inspire her. And, perhaps, the two might even become friends, the suggestion always accompanied by a smile and a fluttering of the right eyelash.

Improving his fluency in French had been one of the excuses that Peter used with his parents, friends, and faculty advisor to justify the year in Paris. Twice a day, morning and evening, Mme Garneau's presence at her sentry post would have offered the opportunity for protracted conversations. But each time he approached the front door to leave or return home, his heart raced for fear of getting trapped by her.

He tiptoed down the final steps, grateful once again for the noiseless complicity of their well-worn marble. The weighty oak door was not as accommodating. The brass handle cooperated, but the ancient hinges protested and a screech bounced up the stairwell and ricocheted back down. Sensing his advantage might be fleeting, Peter flung the door open, leapt across the threshold, and scurried out onto the sidewalk. He sprinted along Avenue Duquesne and slipped around the corner. The view of the tranquilly ornate dome of Les Invalides offered a respite from the throaty "M. Sinclair … Bonjour, Pierre … Emilia viens …" pursuing him.

As Peter passed under the entrance arch of the Sorbonne, he found the usually tranquil courtyard reverberating with as much noise as the crowded street outside. People filled the quadrangle, shouting back and forth. Student leaders exhorted the assembled, their words only passably discernable through the megaphones. Briefcases, tethered piles of books, and bicycles were strewn on the cobblestones. Clusters of youth crouched down arguing over the wording for signs they were preparing. Peter meandered around reading the slogans: "L'ennui est contre-révolutionnaire"; "L'imagination prend le pouvoir!"; "Adieu, de Gaulle!"

With so much of the school involved in organizing the demonstration, his morning class would likely be cancelled. He could go directly to the library without worrying about incurring yet another reprimand for absenteeism.

"Pierre!" There were a hundred Pierres in the courtyard. Without looking up, he scurried toward the exit. "Boston Pierre!" That narrowed the field. The cacophony bouncing off the walls continued to intensify. Keeping a steady pace, he gave no indication of having heard himself being called. In another moment, he was slipping out onto the street.

Peter hurried along rue Saint-Jacques a couple of blocks to get out of range and took a right at rue Soufflot. He crossed the street, dropped his bag beside a lamppost, leaned up against it, and folded his arms. It was still hours before Jean-François's shift. For ten minutes, Peter watched the other waiters moving in and out of the café. This proximity to where Jean-François would be was satisfaction enough for the time being. He picked up his bag and headed to the library.

On postcards home, Peter enthused about the university and his implied involvement in the French political activism that was as intense as the Vietnam protests on American campuses. But his enrolment at the Sorbonne was largely pragmatic. He needed to be registered in order to open the doors of heaven. His primary goal for the year in Paris was to access the sanctity, quietude, and literary opulence of la Bibliothèque Sainte-Geneviève.

Fifteen minutes after the close call in the quadrangle, he walked through the library's modest entrance door, flashed the attendant his ID, and made his way up the stairway and into the anything-but-modest reading room.

He paused, as always, to take it in. A young arms-entwined couple bumped into him. He moved to the side, out of the traffic flow. An elderly woman shuffled by, a worn leather satchel buffeting against her weathered wool coat. A bespectacled balding professor, head buried in a book, navigated with well-honed radar to an empty chair. Two tittering girls glided to a table in a far corner.

A chair scratched the floor to Peter's right. He looked over as a student jumped up, grabbed his scattered papers, and stuffed them into a bag. Peter hurried over to take his place.

A seat like this near the end of the room was his preferred location. From here, he could gaze up and take in Henri Labrouste's awesome 1850 masterpiece—the slender cast-iron ionic columns down the middle of the massive rectangular room anchoring the ornamentally designed iron arches that supported two soaring plaster vaults; the four walls topped by large curved opaque windows yielding at the base to countless shelves of books. Before stepping on the plane, he had read three articles on the library's history, architecture, and collection.

Peter quietly placed his bag on the floor, gently sat in the chair, folded his hands together on the table before him, and raised his head in a deliberately measured pace, moving his gaze from the deeply grained, stained, and scratched table surface up to a horizontal position to take in the brass pedestal lamp with classic alabaster shade fixed in the middle of the table, then further up to the endless rows of triple shelves holding the books that were the repository of so much he wanted to learn, and finally stretching his head back to view the majestic sweep of the double-vaulted ceiling extending from his seat to the frosted arched windows at the far end, through which light cascaded from an outside world a million kilometres away.

This was his daily devotional. Today, as usual, he sat quietly and breathed deeply, letting his gaze meander back and forth along the length of bookshelves, and giving thanks not only for the gods enshrined therein—the Voltaires and the Prousts, the Kierkegaards and the Hegels, the Socrateses and the Sartres—but also for the privilege of direct and unmediated discourse with them. No intermediary was required to ascend a pulpit and read to him from the sacred texts. He could hold these bibles in his own hands and commune with the authors.

Peter chuckled to himself at the overblown romanticism of this imagery.

His access was not quite so immediate. For one thing, his French still needed a lot of work. He reached down into his bag and pulled out an increasingly worn *Larousse French–English Dictionary* and placed it on the table. Then he got up out of his chair and headed to the banks of card catalogues, picked up one of the little green forms, took a stubby pencil from the tray, retraced his steps from earlier days this week to the file drawer he needed, filled out the required information, and then dropped the card into the basket on the librarian's desk. A three-foot wrought iron rail fence separated the reading tables from the bookshelves. Only the high priesthood were allowed to move amongst the stacks. While he was waiting, Peter wandered down the length of the room, crossed over to the opposite side, and sauntered back, surreptitiously glancing at what books other readers had in front of them.

On his return from a second stroll around the library, his book was waiting for him on the pickup desk: *Lettres d'Abélard et d'Héloïse*. He picked it up and smiled appreciatively at the elderly hunchback courier who, clearly winded, had just set down an armful of books requested by other readers. The old man smiled back for the few seconds' break that he took, leaning over and resting his fists on the table. Then he was off with another handful of the little green forms.

Back at his seat, Peter opened his notebook and scanned yesterday's entries until he found the page where he had left off. It was no mystery to him why he was attracted to the letters between Abélard and Héloïse. They were amongst the most prominent of medieval intellectuals, and their lifelong relationship remained the epitome of articulate, passionate, and tortured romance. So much resonated with his interests, his despairs, and his aspirations for a love as intense as theirs. He adored the concept of Abélard—a rigorous and brilliant intellect who had a catholic fascination with all things philosophical and theological, and self-confidence sufficient to challenge established authority and withstand their repeated assaults. Yet for all that evident rationality of mind, Abélard was also endowed with a heart capable of passionate abandon. Then to have found a kindred spirit in Héloïse—a match to his intellect, a response to his sexual lust, and a complement to his capacity for profound human love—was a blessing almost beyond imagination.

Yet, Abélard was more than a concept and Héloïse was more than a fantasy. They were real. They had lived. They had written these beautifully painful letters to each other. From that reality Peter took sustenance.

Not that he wished to emulate their life in every detail—Abélard's castration by Héloïse's furious uncle being a case in point.

Peter flipped the pages in his Larousse repeatedly as he worked through Abélard's "Lettre III." He was frustrated that his French was not yet good enough to luxuriate in the poetry and pathos of Abélard's text without having to constantly consult the dictionary. As tedious as having to translate the French was, it paled in comparison to the Everest he would have had to climb if he had followed through on his original grandiose plan to read their letters in the original Latin. He had excelled in high school Latin, but that was five years ago and he hadn't cracked a Latin text since. Besides, reading the politics of Cicero hadn't prepared him particularly well for the passion of Abélard and Héloïse.

Peter's brow, already furrowed by the challenging line he was trying to decipher, contracted further as a possible translation occurred to him and then skittered elusively away. He picked up his pen and wrote as much of it as he could retrieve, and then he stared at it, biting his lower lip and squinting his right eye, as if that would make it more plausible. He scratched out the phrase and flipped opened his dictionary for the umpteenth time. He sucked on the rubber end of his pencil as he scanned down the selected page. His eyes suddenly lit up, and he rewrote the sentence. Now it read, "Suffer me to avoid destruction, I entreat you by our former tender affection and by our now common misfortune." He smiled from ear to ear, his translating success momentarily trumping his sympathy for the depth of Abélard's angst.

After hours of reading and translating, a series of querulous growls began to erupt from his stomach and, to Peter's embarrassed perception, seemed to fill the cavernous room. He looked at his watch and was shocked to see it was almost 5pm. No wonder his stomach was in protest. He usually had a bite to eat between morning classes and afternoons spent in the library. Skipping class today disrupted this routine. And now he had been so immersed in conversation with Abélard and Héloïse that he had completely forgotten to have lunch.

He closed his notebook with a sigh. He closed *Lettres d'Abélard et d'Héloïse* with a deeper sigh. Catching himself, he glanced up to see if nearby seatmates were watching him. There were fewer chairs occupied at this hour, and none of the readers in his vicinity were paying any attention to him. He rested his hands on the fraying cover and ran his digit lovingly over the embossed title:

"Abélard." *O to have even a fraction of the intellectual capacity of the man,* he moaned to himself. *"Et d'Héloïse." Imagine being one half of a couple linked by an et. To have that other with whom you could discuss the most complex subject and who would respond with insights that enriched your own understanding beyond where you could go alone. And then, my God, to be able to take that other to bed and make love with passionate, raucous energy.*

A shiver ran up and down Peter's spine and then morphed from chilly to warm and traversed his body, aiming for his groin. He returned his gaze to the book cover. *"Lettres d'." To be able to put into words with such precision and poetry those philosophical, theological, and spiritual reflections, let alone the passion, and to be so respected that generations of scholars preserved those writings, allowing them to be read at this desk in la Bibliothèque Sainte-Geneviève 800 years later!*

Only a few diehards sat outside Café Soufflot braving the damp chilliness. Peter headed inside and claimed a banquette seat below a shelf of dusty Albert Camus books. He had placed himself here for the past few weeks in the hope that Camus might be the pimp that eventually connected him and Jean-François. He slipped off his jacket and draped it over the chair on the other side of the table, a discouragement to anyone who might think to occupy it. A moment later, Peter propped himself up, balanced his calves against the base of the bench, reached across the table, extracted his scarf from the coat sleeve, wrapped it around his neck, and sat back down again.

A young waiter Peter had never seen before headed toward his table. "Sébastien!" He stopped midstride and turned toward the bar. Jean-François came out from around the end of the counter and brushed past him, jerking his head in the direction of the kitchen as he passed. Sébastien shrugged and headed away.

Jean-François approached Peter's table, napkin draped over his forearm, glass of water and menu on his tray. He stopped in front of Peter and placed the water and menu on the table. He paused, dropped his hand onto the back of the chair, rested it on Peter's coat, and looked directly into Peter's eyes for the first time in the three months that Peter had been coming to Café Soufflot.

"Bonjour," he said quietly. "Je m'appelle Jean-François."

Peter had fantasized many types of encounters with Jean-François. How to conduct a first conversation was not one of them. "Umm, Peter ... I mean Pierre ... pardon, je m'appelle Pierre."

Jean-François glanced down at where his hand rested on Peter's coat. Cupping his fingers around the collar, he slid his thumb back and forth along the faux fur. Peter fumbled for a pen in his pocket, flipped the cardboard Café Soufflot coaster over, and scribbled his name and address on the back. He slid it across the table. Jean-François stared at it but didn't move to pick it up.

"Garçon?"

Jean-François grimaced and shot a glance at a table nearby. "Un moment," he said brusquely.

He released his grip on Peter's coat and hesitated, hand suspended above the table.

"Garçon, garçon!"

He snatched up the coaster and shoved it into his apron pocket.

"Ce soir?" Jean-François asked, burrowing his eyes into Peter's. Peter nodded. "Je pourrais te visiter à vingt-deux heures, plus or moins." Peter nodded. "Maintenant, comme d'habitude, soupe à l'oignon et un verre de vin rouge?" Peter nodded.

Jean-François left and attended to the other table.

Peter started breathing again.

Midway through taking the patron's order, Jean-François excused himself, returned to Peter, and reached out his hand. Peter took it and they shook hands.

"Bon," Jean-François said. And then, in English, he said, "It's nice to meet you. Finally."

Peter did a double take. Jean-François smiled. "I spent time in the United States. I have an MFA from Cornell."

———— ⌇ ————

The persistent whirr of the electric heater fan contrasted with their erratic breathing as they gradually came down. Peter had buried his head in the pillow to muffle his climax screams. Jean-François was cradling Peter, depositing silent kisses on the top of his head, which was nestled against his shoulder. They had yet to speak a word to each other. Mutually awkward smiles had been exchanged when Peter opened the door to Jean-François's knock. Peter held out his hand and Jean-François took it, an echo of the handshake at the café hours earlier. But this time, neither let go. Peter pulled Jean-François into his room. From that moment on, they maintained physical contact, through the disrobing, the move to the bed, and during their lovemaking, as if to break contact risked shattering a precious fragility.

Peter freed his right arm from where it was starting to cramp, squeezed between his sweating body and the rough plaster wall. He fingered the black hairs on Jean-François's arm. "I wasn't sure you'd come." Peter turned and looked Jean-François in the eyes. He raised his head and kissed his lips with a quick, self-consciously noncommittal peck, and then rested back on his shoulder.

Someone yanked the toilet chain brusquely in the corridor. Cascading water squealed through the pipes and could be heard splashing across the floor of the water closet. Peter whispered, "You never seemed to notice me at the café. Until this afternoon."

"That's what you thought."

"And you were so late. I thought maybe … you had changed your mind."

"I almost didn't make it here tonight because of the armed sentry at your door downstairs."

Peter scrambled out of Jean-François's embrace, squatted on

his haunches, and said, "Oh my God, I forgot that I had to unlock the door for you. How did you get in?"

"Your dear concierge was still on duty."

"Oh. Sorry. Did she tell you about her war wound?"

"Yes, and that was helpful. I launched into a long discourse of the role of writers in the French resistance during the war."

"Including Camus?" Peter smiled.

"Bien sûr. I eventually exhausted her. She let me in after I had convinced her that I was your tutor."

Peter leaned back against the wall and stretched his legs out over the bed, resting them at right angles across Jean-François's. Jean-François placed one hand on Peter's knee. His other hand nonchalantly fingered his own still semierect penis. Peter watched as Jean-François scanned the room, his eyes moving from the cold-water sink over to the frost-covered window and then stopping and squinting at the books on the small table that served as Peter's desk. They both shivered at the same moment. Peter reached down, took hold of the duvet that their thrashing had pushed to the bottom of the bed, and pulled it up to cover both their bodies. Jean-François, his head tilted as he tried to read the titles on the spines of the books piled on the desk, said, "So what is it that you're studying here in Paris that I'm supposed to be your tutor for?"

"Officially, I'm in a program at the Sorbonne for foreign students. Cours de langue et civilisation française. But I'm really here to spend the year reading, and hopefully try my hand at writing. I virtually live at la Bibliothèque Sainte-Geneviève, around the corner from your café."

Jean-François looked back at Peter. "Il n'est-ce pas *mon* café."

"I mean where … you're working … where we met."

"Est-ce que nous devons parler français?"

"We could. We should." Peter's fluency in French diminished when he was tired. At this point, he was very tired. "Tell me about yourself. What did you study in the States?"

"Il y a longtemps," Jean-François said quietly. He turned his head back toward the desk. "Almost 15 years ago. American literature and creative writing."

"That's fantastic. So you're a writer?"

Jean-François grimaced and disappeared.

"There's so much we could talk about." Peter sought gamely to pull Jean-François back.

After a few minutes, Jean-François mumbled, "Il faut que je parte." He extracted his legs from underneath Peter's and sat upright on the edge of the bed. Stretching his leg out, he planted his heel on top of his discarded pants on the floor, maneuvered them toward the bed, fished inside a pocket, and retrieved his watch. "Il faut que je parte."

"Can't you stay the night, Jean-François? Please?"

Jean-François looked at the desk and then back at Peter.

"C'est trop tard." He fingered his watch as he stared through Peter. The muscles around his mouth tautened. "Trop tard. Pour tout cela."

Peter watched him dress.

Jean-François let himself out without looking back.

———

Peter entered through the massive wooden doorway just as the first chords of the 45-minute pre-Mass recital reverberated through Notre Dame's Gothic nave. As was his custom, he headed toward the left aisle and took a seat at the end of one of the rows about two-thirds of the way back from the chancel. He placed his coat on the woven wicker seat of the chair beside him, thought better of it, and moved it down onto the marble floor.

The organist made his way through a variety of selections from the Baroque to the contemporary. For Peter, the older, the better. Usually. The familiarity of Buxtehude or Bach was conducive to his reflective mood at this point on most Sundays. Sunday afternoons were spent in the Louvre because admission was free. When he initially established this pattern several months ago, the jostling crowds had frustrated him. But over time, he had found out-of-the way rooms with pre-Renaissance masters that intrigued him and, apparently, were of little interest to most tourists. There he would begin his contemplative afternoons, later progressing to Notre Dame for the recital and Mass.

But today his mood was far from contemplative and the cacophonous modern pieces were in sync with his agitation. There had been no sign of Jean-François for the past week at the café. Sébastien had served him, with marked surliness. Peter tried not to read too much into his attitude. Peter threw himself into his coursework and reading at the library. He even participated in one of the student-led antigovernment protests.

"Come on, Betty, let's sit here." The southwestern drawl broke over Peter's shoulder as a half dozen Au Printemps and Galeries Lafayette shopping bags grazed his knees. "'Scuse me, son, can we get by you?" Peter, whose gaze had been focused on the scraped marble flooring worn down by generations of parishioners, watched a western boot implant a soggy stain on his coat sleeve. The space between him and the row of seats ahead was too constrained by the shuffling past of Betty and hubby, and their winter coats and shopping bags, for Peter to grab his coat before it suffered more footprints. Once the two of them had settled in chairs on his right, Peter reached down, picked up his coat, and vigorously brushed off the sleeve. "Ain't this marvellous, Bet? Gettin' to attend Mass in Paris's bloody Nodder Damm."

Coat in hand, Peter stood up and made his way to the back of the cathedral, moving against the flow of traffic. He headed across the nave, moved down the right aisle, and slipped into a seat next to one of the massive pillars.

Mass began. Peter shifted in his chair so he could lean up against the pillar. Resting his head on the cold stone, he let the words and music wash over him, anticipating the eventual arrival of the familiar rhythms of the Eucharist liturgy. What he always attended to the most was nothing verbal or musical but was rather the tinkling of the small bells by one of the assisting priests as the host and the wine were elevated, silence throughout the cathedral except for this high-pitched simplicity.

There was a sad sweetness to it for Peter, a moment of visceral longing.

The sound conjured up in Peter's mind the TV image of Walt Disney's Tinkerbell darting out from behind the castle's spiralled pinnacle and scattering fairy dust from the end of her wand—his 6-year-old self sitting cross-legged inches from the TV screen in his parents' home as Tinkerbell smiled directly at him and him alone, and then blessed him with her magic sparkles.

Chairs and feet shuffled near him as people rose to join the procession toward the chancel. Peter slipped on his coat and made his way to the aisle, merging into the line, head bowed. He stared down at the fraying seam of a grey cloth coat worn by the elderly parishioner progressing slowly forward in front of him. He glanced up at the back of the person's head. A wool-knit toque covered the head to within an inch or so of the neck, exposing a few strands of hair. Peter couldn't tell if it was a man or a woman. To satisfy his curiosity, he stepped to the side so he could see more of the person's head and, in so doing, intruded into the line of people returning from having been served. A woman cleared her throat, gruffly signalling to Peter to move. "Pardon," he murmured, looking into a set of displeased eyes. She moved past and was followed by a young girl dressed in a chequered overcoat and matching beret. Peter caught the bright smile on her face—such a contrast to the annoyed woman ahead of her. The girl's sparkling eyes looked up adoringly at her father, whose left hand she held. The father's right hand trailed after him, clasping the hand of a young boy so similar in stature that Peter thought the boy and girl might be twins. Peter looked up at the father to offer a congratulatory smile on the adorability of his children.

He froze in his tracks.

So did Jean-François.

Grumblings erupted in both lines as they stood staring at each other, impeding the flow of traffic.

A woman holding the other hand of the young boy and bringing up the rear of the family jerked her head back and forth, glaring at Peter, scowling at Jean-François. "Cheri, allons," she said in a tone at odds with the endearment used.

Jean-François turned away from Peter and left. Again.

The light slowly dissipated. Only the windows on the west side of la Bibliothèque Sainte-Geneviève retained any lustre, and even they held little more than a grey paleness. Another 10 minutes and all the windows would be dark, sealing shut the outside world. By contrast, the interior grew in warmth as the table lamps asserted their now indispensable role of providing light for the readers, illumination that was softened and enriched by the alabaster shades.

The book was open to the final letter from Abélard to Héloïse. Moving back and forth between text and dictionary, Peter wrote, scribbled out, reordered, rewrote, and then put his pen down, lodging it between the pages before closing his notebook. He sat back and looked around the library, scanning the teeming shelves and summoning enthusiasm for launching into the works of another author, a different era, a contrasting genre.

That would be tomorrow's decision.

He reopened his notebook and read his just-finished entry: "Let us no more deceive ourselves with remembrance of our past pleasures; we but make our lives troubled and spoil the sweets of solitude."

References

Abélard, Pierre, and Héloïse Abélard. *The Letters of Abélard and Héloïse.* Ed. by Michael Clancy. Trans. by Betty Radice. London: Penguin Books, 1974.

Camus, Albert. *L'étranger.* Paris: Gallimard, 1942.

fifth business fiction

LIKE GETTING TANGLED UP WITH MOTHER'S sticky flypaper.

Robertson Davies laid his pen down on the cover of his September 1959 notebook. As a child he had watched as one of the flytrap rolls that his mother used to tack to the ceiling during the summer came loose and fell. Instinctively, he had reached out to grab it. Bad move. At first it was only his thumb and index finger trapped in the clutches of the gluey strip. Before long, his other hand was ensnared, and then the contraption wrapped itself around his arm like a boa constrictor.

Recently, a winter village street image had surfaced in his mind. It now stuck to him, like the flypaper of his childhood, recurring with increasing frequency and, on each occasion, in greater detail. It was so persistent he had come to the conclusion that he'd better yield. It was demanding to be written about.

He ran his fingers around the edges of the notebook as he played with the image in his mind, letting the clarity fade in and fade out. After a few moments, he opened his notebook and wrote as follows:

> *In a small town a young parson is taking his pregnant wife for an evening walk. Two boys are playing nearby in the snow, the one bullying the other. The frailer one tolerates*

117

> *it because he idolizes the assertive boy.*
> *The mischievous boy throws a snowball*
> *in which there is a rock. Intended for his*
> *playmate, it instead hits the woman on*
> *the head, hurting her seriously. When the*
> *child is born (prematurely?), she loses her*
> *reason: after a period of caring for her at*
> *home, she is sent to an asylum.*

Davies set his pen down, swivelled the large leather chair, and looked out the window to the right of his desk. Moonlight was filtering through the trees. Before long, the leaves would turn colour and fall, and more light would hit the yard—the chillier, paler light of the changing season.

He glanced down at what he had written and was momentarily distracted, admiring his beautiful penmanship. He rolled the scene around in his mind.

He picked up his pen and wrote a few more notes:

> *Revenge would be the theme—revenge*
> *against the boy who threw the snowball, but*
> *revenge not exacted by the parson for the*
> *impact on his wife but by the son whose*
> *premature birth was precipitated by the*
> *callous aggression.*

Davies pushed the chair away from the desk and walked over to the far wall. He swept his eyes along the rows of books on the shelves but attended to none. The winter village scene was all that registered. He tugged at it, prodding for details, motives, consequences. It had been badgering him for days, erupting in his mind on the weekend when he was pulling weeds in the garden, and again today when he was lugging furniture around at the Peterborough *Examiner* office where he worked as editor and publisher and wrote the *Diary of Samuel Marchbanks*, required reading by everyone in town to see which local foibles and thinly disguised personalities were being skewered that week.

He looked at his watch. It was almost 11, just about time to join Brenda for the usual drink, snack, and end-of-the-day conversation. One of their regular topics these days was how lonely in, and bored by, Peterborough they were.

Peterborough, for its part, was uneasy around them. Robertson with his prodigious beard and formal Edwardian blazer and flannels struck an intimidating pose as he strode daily from home to office and around town. Brenda, having abandoned hopes of a professional acting career at marriage, carried herself with a grace that seemed to hover somewhere between hauteur and flamboyancy. And yet, the citizens' expectations that their eccentric artistic residents would live an eccentric artistic lifestyle didn't materialize. Robertson chuckled to himself as he recalled June Callwood's profile in *Maclean's* magazine in which she observed the following:

> The appearance of Davies and his actress wife, who dresses like a ladylike gypsy, led the people of Peterborough to expect something exceptional, like opium parties and orgies on the lawn. Disappointingly, the Davieses are the most circumspect couple in Peterborough.

The citizens, aware of his rising public profile to the higher echelons of Canadian letters, would have been astonished that such disappointment had an echo of sorts in those late-night conversations inside the Davies's house. Robertson would admit to almost no one other than Brenda his nagging self-doubts and unrealized hopes and ambitions. He had expected, assumed, that by the time he reached middle age he would have accomplished much more professionally and for his family.

He wondered whether this new story idea might be the tipping point. He stood for a few more moments, staring at the volumes of plays, novels, and reference books sagging on the wooden shelves. He pivoted around, crossed the room, and sat back down in his chair.

He envied those people who complained of writer's block. His was the opposite problem. In this initial discovery stage there was so much material building up around the kernel of the idea that he had to struggle to make something comprehensible of it. Picking up the notebook, he scanned what he had already written, turned the page, and pressed his index finger down the spine so that the paper lay flat. He wrote two more pages' worth of notes about the parson whose life revolves so much around his lovely young wife that her injuries from the snowball unhinge him, tensions caused by the varying social statuses of the characters, and rivalries within and amongst the community's churches.

Davies closed the notebook. The story was started. He was far from having any idea what it might be called, and quite sure that it would take the form of a novel. There were many complicated relationships and plot developments to work out. But the whole thing had begun to come to life—the characters and their situations and what lay behind it all.

He opened the door of his study and headed into the hallway. "I'm coming, Brenda."

Davies scanned the cluttered downstairs rooms of impresario Nicholas Goldschmidt's sumptuous Toronto home teeming with people and paper, music and mayhem. Planning for the Centennial Spectacle was seriously behind schedule. Six months to C-day and counting. A who's who of the Canadian artistic community had been recruited to plan a massive open-air pageant to be staged on Parliament Hill during the 1967 summer of Canada's centennial.

Composer Louis Applebaum sat at the piano playing his way through his musical score. Goldschmidt, who had been named choral director, was leaning over Applebaum's shoulder and following along, his right hand conducting an imaginary mega-concert band and mass choir, and his left hand scribbling pencil notes in the margins.

Robertson studied the costume and stage set sketches that Marie Day and Murray Laufer had prepared. He had laid them out on the dining room table and now lifted one after another to scrutinize every detail, visualizing how they would wow the thousands of spectators. He liked what he saw. Davies had written the script for the extravaganza. His draft was a grandiose scenario to depict Canada's history, present, and future.

Tyrone Guthrie, the founding director of the Stratford Festival who had been enlisted to direct the whole centennial affair, stretched the telephone cord around the corner into the dining room as he negotiated on the phone with an Ottawa mandarin. "Damn right it will work. I'm looking at the mock-ups now." He cupped his hand over the receiver and said, "Robbie, now they're telling me that they don't want the stage to obstruct the view of the Queen's arrival. Idiots!"

Davies rolled his eyes. "For God's sake Tony, they're already paying us nothing and yet demanding the impossible. Tell that minion in Public Works that if they give us much more grief, I'll never write for patriot reasons again. I've got more gratifying projects on which I could be spending my time."

Fifth Business was one such project, but *gratifying* was an overstatement for how Davies had been feeling about the long-pondered tale. Over the years, he had come up with ideas and a possible scheme of construction. He had tried to start writing. A page and a half in, he gave up. The story had not yet been ready to be written. Or he was not yet ready to write it. Either way, further gestation was required.

The small matter of establishing Massey College had been

the main impediment interfering with work on *Fifth Business*. Davies had received a summons on New Year's Eve 1960 from Vincent Massey, former governor-general and scion of one of the preeminent Canadian establishment families, to come to his home. There he was presented with the offer to be the first master of a new residential college for male graduate students that the Massey Foundation was creating as a gift to the University of Toronto. On occasion over the next few years, Davies came close to regretting his decision to accept when the workload and fractious politics of building and organizing Massey College got almost overwhelming. But the lure was irresistible for Robertson and Brenda—to escape Peterborough and move to Toronto, living once again amongst their intellectual and artistic peers.

Tyrone shuffled back into the parlour, barking Davies's threat into the phone as he walked. Louis had stopped playing the piano. With Nicholas now sitting beside him on the piano bench, the two of them were both writing notes on the music score stretched across their laps. Davies walked around the table studying the set designs from various angles, brainstorming how the stage and bleachers might be reconfigured to maximize visibility of the royals.

In the momentary lull, Brenda's laugh slipped from the parlour into the dining room. Davies looked up, admiring how classically elegant she looked. Their eyes met.

Brenda winked at Robertson. *What a partnership we have*, Brenda mused. *In addition to everything else, I think that any man who can make his wife laugh at breakfast is a marvellous husband.* She giggled at her own jest.

Robertson's curiosity was piqued. He made his way into the parlour, took hold of her hand, and drew her away from the cluster of people with whom she had been talking. He led her into the kitchen and dropped her hand, only to pick up a bottle of wine on the counter and pour them each a fresh glass. He handed one to her, and they clinked glasses.

Brenda watched Robertson sip the wine, his eyes no longer on hers but wandering off, nowhere specific, somewhere internal. She recognized the distracted stare. "What are you thinking about?" she asked quietly.

"I have a premonition that this whole effort"—he waved his hand toward the dining room and parlour—"is going to come to naught."

"Really? You are all getting along so well."

"Oh, we are. The problem lies with the bureaucratic imbeciles in Ottawa. They are a different matter, an inhuman—one might say reptilian—species with no appreciation for what makes for great theatre and art. No, I take that back. My characterization does a disservice to the noble, slithering, ground-hugging saurians of God's good creation."

Brenda almost spilled her wine as one hand flew to her mouth to stifle a guffaw.

"I think I'm ready to get back to *Fifth Business.*" Davies threw his head back and laughed. "Maybe Nicholas's house is charmed. I'm here thinking that I may be ready to start working on the novel in earnest—and it was here in this very kitchen that you gave me the title for it."

"I did?"

"Yes, a few years ago we were here for one reason or another and you overheard a theatrical friend ... I don't think you ever told me whom ... telling an anecdote about an aging European opera singer talking about operatic roles in her youth."

"That's right," Brenda said. "Oh, who was that again? But I do remember what she was describing. The heroes and heroines in opera are, of course, sung by sopranos and tenors; the villains and temptresses, by basses and contraltos. Then, there is what they called *fifth business*—the sort of roles sung by other singers whose parts were necessary to the plot but not central to it."

Robertson leaned in and kissed Brenda lightly on the cheek. "I was delighted by the idea and the phrase. It works perfectly."

"Well," Brenda said as she stood on her toes to reciprocate the peck on Robertson's cheek, "here's to *Fifth Business*." They clinked glasses again.

"Now, there's the small matter of writing the bloody thing," Davies growled.

———

The noise that ricocheted around the high-ceilinged dining hall at Massey College made conversation difficult at the best of times. Davies was getting frustrated. He wanted to tell McClelland of his progress on *Fifth Business*.

Now a junior fellow had approached. His arms resting on the edge of the table and leaning in toward Davies, he spoke rapidly, sensing Robertson's growing annoyance with the interruption.

Davies sipped a spoonful of soup and then lifted his head up to look at, and then past, the anxious young scholar. He fixed his gaze on a short phrase in the long George Santayana quote he had selected to be inscribed around the dining hall ceiling: "Learned your place in the world." *I clearly have more work to do on that virtue with this young one*, Davies thought.

Breaking into the graduate student's summarizing of his thesis idea midsentence, Davies said, "There are possibilities in your proposal on Shaw's gender philosophy, but you are overlooking one of his other key dictums, that 'there is no sincerer love than the love of food,' and at the moment you are depriving the eminent Canadian publisher Jack McClelland"—Davies saluted his dining companion across the table with half a spoonful of soup, to which McClelland responded with a gracious titling of his head in acknowledgment—"and me from savouring that sensuous pleasure which was held in such esteem by the inestimable George Bernard. Please make an office appointment, as all others know is the protocol, and I will be more than happy to discuss at length your proposal to ensure that neither you"—spoon directed toward the student—"nor this hallowed institution that we have so recently birthed"—spoon raised toward the ceiling and moved around to encompass the hall and, in the process, splattering the table with droplets of split pea—"nor I as your humble advisor is unduly embarrassed by a substandard piece of scholarship."

"I'm so sorry, sir," the student stuttered as he backed away from the table. "Most inconsiderate of me." The student bowed as he stepped back, his bum bumping into the next table. Straightening up, he glanced back and forth between the two, said, "I apologize, so sorry, excuse me," and scurried toward the dining hall exit.

"God, they're a dull lot," Davies mumbled.

McClelland watched as Robertson resumed eating, swiping his napkin across his upper and lower lips to remove any soup residue that might have clung to his prodigious moustache and beard. McClelland ventured, "That was a bit brutal, wasn't it, Robbie?"

"Pfft. He should have known better. Or he should know that he should have known better."

McClelland raised his eyebrows.

Davies leaned in and whispered, "I strongly suspect that he's a poofter, that he sucks cock."

McClelland coughed and covered his mouth. "Ah, homosexual, you mean. Well, isn't sucking cock what they do?"

Robertson's eyes twinkled. "But I hear that he talks about it," he said, relishing the touch of naughtiness within the establishment walls of Massey College. "Don't worry. I'll have a long, and I assure you, most supportive discussion with our young friend once he gets over his embarrassment and summons the courage to make a proper appointment. Unlike most of my colleagues here," he said, not moving his head as he swept his eyes around the rows of chattering tables in the hall, "I'm not one to allow unfettered access with an open office door or, especially, in the midst of lunch. The maintenance of rigorous intellectual standards and traditional academic protocol is of the utmost importance—the civilizing influence of an Oxford or a Cambridge on the University of Toronto campus."

"That commitment being no doubt why the Masseys asked you to help establish the college and to be the founding master."

"Doubtless."

"Ah, Robbie." McClelland laughed. "I've always admired your self-confidence."

Davies did not find anything humorous in his friend's observation. "I've sweated blood and tears over the past five years in establishing Massey College to create just the atmosphere by which young men could gain such self-confidence themselves— not of the preening variety, but of the soul. It's my aspiration that they experience what has motivated me all my life." Davies stared into his soup bowl as into a fathomless pool and continued quietly, saying, "The pursuit of that solitary growth, that continuing search for what is enduring in the Self, from which all the great loves, all the high adventures, and all the noble rewards of life have their beginning."

The racket in the room made it difficult for McClelland to catch every word.

Davies suddenly looked up and said, "Speaking of which, I'm writing again and bloody pleased with it."

"What do you mean, 'writing again'? You're always writing."

Davies scowled as he set his spoon down. Looking directly at McClelland, he said, "Yes, I'm always writing about others. But the fact of the matter is that I want to be a Canadian writer, rather than a writer about Canadian writers. Now five years on from our 1963 opening, Massey College is firmly established and functioning well. I've dispensed with most of the academic writing to which I had committed myself. So now ..."

Davies wrapped his right hand around his spoon handle and grabbed his fork with his other fist. He pounded both fists down on the table five times in quick succession. The metal-on-wood noise cracked like a whip through the hall. Davies pretended to ignore all the heads that simultaneously riveted in his direction and the silence that severed the previous commotion. He threw his head back and roared with laughter, and then just as suddenly he leaned halfway across the table, beaded McClelland with his eyes, and in full voice declared, "And now, I'm writing for myself again, Jack. And loving it. *Fifth Business*."

A hushed atmosphere descended on the hall after the master's theatrical outburst. Davies dropped his voice again, but this time McClelland could hear every word.

"*Fifth Business* is something of a spiritual autobiography in fact." He fixed McClelland with a gaze that brooked no sarcastic rebuttal. "I choose the word *spiritual* with intent, for during the past ten years the things of the spirit have become increasingly important to me. Not in a churchy sense but in what I must call a Jungian sense. That may make you laugh, or spit ..." Davies watched McClelland for any reaction. His friend sat motionless, and so he continued. "Through Jung's ever-thickening veils of thought and fantasy, I discern something that gives great richness to my life and helps me to behave rather more decently toward other people than my unaided inspiration can achieve. And that is important to me: the world is so full of self-seekers, crooks, and sons of bitches that I am very keen to be a decent man—not a Holy Joe or a do-gooder, but a man who does not gag every time he looks into the mirror."

The dining hall had begun to clear, students and faculty alike giving a wide berth to the table at which Davies and McClelland sat.

"And that's what informs my writing of *Fifth Business*. I've finished the first two sections in those precious hours squeezed in between my teaching and my responsibilities as master here. Twenty-five thousand words and counting. Brenda and I will have use of a country house next summer, where I'll write most of the rest."

With meticulous precision, Davies gently laid the utensils

back down beside his plate, smiled broadly, and said, "Bloody impressive. Eh?"

Jack McClelland lifted his water glass and held it over the table toward Davies. "A toast to Robertson Davies. A Canadian writer."

Davies lifted his water glass up, clinked McClelland's, and said, "To Robertson Davies. The Canadian writer."

———— ⌣ ————

The trunk of a large tree rested on the ground at about a 45-degree angle to the stream. Davies walked around the upended root ball. Enough of the root tentacles remained lodged in the ground to sustain life in some of the branches that hung suspended just feet above the babbling brook. Clusters of leaves swayed in the breeze, glistening with water pellets tossed up from below.

He pulled the gardening gloves out of his back pocket, whisked them across a section of the bark, turned around, and sat down on the trunk, wiggling his bum around for a few moments to get more comfortable. He crossed his arms and closed his eyes, listening to the stream lapping over the rocks complemented by the cicadas' sounds resonating down the creek valley. Though sitting in a shady area, he felt the sun-warmed breeze against his face diminished only slightly by the coolness of the creek. He drew a handkerchief from his pocket and dabbed the sweat on his forehead and cheeks. Miscalculating as he went to stuff it back in his trousers, he saw the handkerchief slip down onto the ground and land at his feet.

As he was about to reach down to retrieve it, he noticed an almost perfectly round stone with the circumference of a nickel amongst the pebbles that lined the water's edge. With the toe of his shoe, he manipulated it over onto his white handkerchief. Bracing his hands on the truck so that he didn't lose his balance, he used both feet to lift the edges of the handkerchief until they covered the stone. He bent over and picked up the handkerchief and wrapped it further into a ball, the stone securely hidden in the middle.

Davies raised his arm above his head and, grasping the crumpled handkerchief firmly in his palm, mimicked tossing it at a target on the other side of the creek. Finally after a decade of ruminating on the winter village scene that had captured his imagination in 1959, he was closing in on completing the manuscript, chronicling the lifelong impacts on four people of a stone hidden in a snowball.

Not four real people. Though they might as well have been.

Dunstan Ramsey, his alter ego. No and yes. Davies looked over his shoulder and could only just see through the trees Brenda's sunhat bobbing as she continued the weeding of the flowerbed around the country house, a joint endeavor from which he had excused himself for this stroll down to the creek. Crotchety history teacher Dunstan Ramsey, persistently plagued by the suspicion that hangs over every bachelor schoolmaster—that he is a homosexual, never married, and never knew the kind of love that Davies felt for Brenda. It struck Davies as counterintuitive that he had moulded this narrator to live a largely loveless life, so foreign to his own experience.

And yet, he was Dunstan Ramsey. Davies turned away from watching Brenda, slightly guiltily, and stared back into the stream. The interior life that he valued so highly felt adulterous at times like this. It was of necessity solitude—time and space free from distractions to think, to pursue intellectual challenges, to create artistic masterworks, and, most of all, to plumb the spiritual depths that so enriched a life of reflection and of creation. He had vested Dunstan Ramsey with much of his own most profound passion.

Dunstan Ramsey's life could hardly have been lived more in the shadows. Percy Boy Staunton's could hardly have been lived more out of them, where he craved and relished wealth and public adoration. Davies felt satisfied with how he had fashioned these two characters to be polar opposites in so many ways and yet inextricably linked from that initial snowball fight through the interweaving of their professional lives to the final dramatic culmination—"my lifelong friend and enemy," as he had Dunstan Ramsey describing Percy Boy Staunton in the second paragraph of the novel.

Would readers intuit a repressed homosexual lust on Dunstan Ramsey's part for athletic, handsome Percy Boy Staunton? Davies thought he knew something of that kind of desire. He had had a crush on another boy in his Upper Canada College student days. Though it was brief, he recalled how powerful it had been and how transgressive it had felt. But more than personal experience, it was Jungian psychology that had given him motifs to use in fashioning his character's personalities, motivations, and actions. Sexual ambiguity wasn't restricted to Dunstan Ramsey. Percy Boy Staunton's endless pursuit of heterosexual conquests carried an undertone of desperation. And there was the culture of "corporate homosexuality" in Staunton's business empire, where he idolized the clean-cut young men whom he employed in his companies, grooming them to be aggressive superior men in the business world, serving him as corporation Ganymedes, only to cast them aside as disappointments when the young men invariably opted to marry an undeserving young woman who would inevitably diminish their chances of unfettered success in the corporate world. And the climax with Staunton's drowned body discovered to have a stone in its mouth—how wonderfully phallic.

Davies tightened his grip on the crumpled handkerchief ball in his right hand. He tossed it into his left hand. In the process, it almost unravelled, the pebble coming close to slipping out. He clenched his fist just in time. A stone encased in a well-compacted snowball is so much more secure, all the worse for poor pregnant Mary Dempster hit on the fateful morning by the snowball thrown by Staunton and intended for Ramsey. Davies loved

Mary Dempster. He felt so badly for how tragedy had dogged her from the resulting concussion and on throughout her life. But it was more than love and pity. He idolized her both literally and metaphorically. Or rather, Dunstan Ramsey did, which was more or less the same thing.

Enter Paul Dempster, born prematurely of the fragile Mary. Davies looked forward to spending a few hours this evening revisiting the writing that he had done this morning on the final scenes. His ordered mind appreciated the symmetry of Paul's framing of the plot by his appearance, initially involuntary at the beginning and then decisively and with retribution at the end. Davies leaned back a bit on the tree trunk, being careful not to lose his balance, and imagined a university English class debating whether he had fashioned Paul's place in the novel in order to create such symmetry or whether the symmetry had emerged organically out of a well-crafted storyline. Maybe a doctoral thesis or two would be written on the topic.

Davies, manoeuvring himself to place both feet back firmly on the ground, braced his hands against the trunk, managing the slight awkwardness of his left hand grasping the handkerchief and stone. Still leaning against the trunk, he stretched his left leg out to rest the heel for a moment just at the water's edge, and then he repeated the stretch with his right leg. Both legs were stiff from the earlier up and down of the gardening.

He grimaced and mumbled to himself. "Perish the thought that my imagination muscles might someday stiffen."

Davies scowled as he walked the short distance from Massey College to the York Club to have drinks with his Canadian and English publishers. A bitter gust of late winter wind swept down St. George Street. He gathered his scarf up to cover more of his face.

Righteous indignation he could do well. He had honed his skills in portraying emotion appropriate to the occasion through his work under Tyrone Guthrie's tutelage at London's Old Vic in the late 1930s and his many subsequent theatrical roles in the United Kingdom and Canada from stage manager to director, playwright to actor, dramaturge to critic. Bombastic was not his preferred style. More powerful was the intensity of an understated tone laced with literate sarcasm—the stage whisper such a potent tool, so underrated.

His performance on this occasion would not rest on acting skill alone. Today, it was personal. He was genuinely piqued.

Fifth Business was a creation in which he had invested not only a great deal of time and energy but also a great deal of himself, of his soul. He resented having to justify the manuscript to publishers.

The rejection by Scribner's in New York had stung. The mixed signals from Macmillan of Canada were confusing. Viking in New York was considering it, as was Macmillan in London. It was now March 1970 and no unequivocal commitment to publish had been received in the four months since he had delivered the final manuscript last December. He assumed that his stature in the world of arts and letters would make it difficult for them to reject *Fifth Business*, even if, as he suspected, some in the CanLit community and beyond considered him passé. But what was galling was the pallid response that he had been getting: "It's very fine—but, of course, there are a few points …"

A dirty moraine of slush about a foot and a half high pushed up by a recent pass of the snowplough blocked Davies's ease of access across Bloor Street. Certain that his foot would sink down into the wet snow if he stepped on it, thereby flooding his galoshes and soaking his shoes and socks, he leapt awkwardly over it onto the street proper. The horn of a car careening past within a few feet sent him stumbling backward. He maintained his balance, but at the cost of a thoroughly soaked right foot.

Davies glared up at the traffic light that he had neglected to consult a moment ago and willed it to turn green. It promptly complied. He trudged across the street, refusing to alter his gait, as most mortals would with one foot dry and the other drenched and cold.

Davies passed the wrought iron fencing and walked up the front walk to the grand building that had housed the York Club for the past 60 years. Owning the largest distillery in the British Empire could buy you a lot of house in the late 19th century. George Gooderham and his wife built their magnificent Romanesque Revival home not only for lavish entertaining but also for the domestic demands of raising a family of 11 children. Davies paused a few feet from the stairs leading to the main entrance and looked up at the peaked turret that anchored the front corner of the building.

The disparity in sensation between his two feet was not the only thing that felt disorienting.

Rearing 11 children in a castle such as this was a world away from the modest house and small family that he had constructed in his imagination for Dunstan Ramsey and his brother to be raised in by their parents, let alone the even more frugal Baptist parsonage in which Mary Dempster gave premature birth to her only child, Paul, aided by Dunstan's mother and overseen by the traumatized Rev. Amasa Dempster. And Toronto was a world away from small-town Deptford, his fictionalized version of Thamesville in southwestern Ontario, where Davies grew up. Though the storyline in *Fifth Business* included settings far removed from Deptford, it was still that rural village scene of the novel's opening section that epitomized the tone of the book in Davies's mind. The dissonance of stepping into this grandiose edifice in downtown Toronto in order to argue for his small-scale novel momentarily unnerved him.

Get a grip, Robbie, he chided himself. *Small-scale in setting maybe, but grand and profound in themes—responsibility, revenge, religion. You've got nothing to apologize for. Now go in there and defend your art.*

At the coat check, Davies dropped his briefcase on the floor, took off his overcoat, and tossed it onto the counter. Steadying himself with one hand on the counter's edge, he started to manipulate his galoshes off his shoes, but then he hesitated and decided against it. "That's all," he said to the clerk as he snatched the coat check tag from the outstretched arm, picked up his briefcase, and headed toward the dining room, partly self-conscious and partly relishing the syncopated sloshing sound produced by his walk.

He found the others seated at a round table near the back of the dining room, the drinks in front of them already partly consumed. "Am I late?" he asked Ramsay Derry, the fiction editor at Macmillan of Canada. "I thought you said five o'clock." Davies fiddled with the sleeves of his suit jacket and shirt to push them up his wrist past his watch. He looked at the time: 5 p.m. on the dot. He turned his arm around, pointing the watch face at each of the others in turn.

Derry was on his feet reaching out to shake Davies's hand. "Yes, yes, five o'clock. I mean, no, you're not late. We just all happened to arrive a bit early."

Davies cocked his head a touch to the side, took Derry's hand, and held it for a moment before shaking it. "Ah, you all happened to arrive a bit early, did you? I see."

"Please, Robertson, have a seat," said Alan Maclean, managing director of Macmillan of London, who was also on his feet, arm outstretched. Davies moved around the table to the vacant chair, propped his briefcase on the floor, leaned it up against the table leg, pulled out the chair, and stood erect between it and the table before reaching his hand out and shaking Maclean's. Everyone resumed sitting.

A waiter unobtrusively placed a tumbler with Davies's preferred whisky brand on the table in front of him and then quietly departed. Davies lifted the glass and took a generous sip. He set it back down and reached over to his briefcase. Unlatching the rusting clasp, he pulled out a large envelope bulging with hundreds of pages of typed manuscript and plopped it down on the table in front of him. Not saying a word, he looked around the table at each of the others in turn, folded his arms across his chest, and waited.

"Well, Rob," Derry said, breaking the silence. "You know … I've already told you … that initially I was a bit anxious about what *Fifth Business* would be like since you had been away from writing novels for some time. But," he said as he shifted his gaze and started addressing Maclean, "I can tell you that by the time that I was 30 or 40 pages into Rob's manuscript, I felt the hairs on the back of my head standing up. I just knew …" He paused and smiled at Davies. "I just knew that his was going to be a wonderful book." Davies smiled back, shrugging his shoulders in an "of course" gesture.

Maclean leapt in with his own praise for the manuscript, though expressed with less enthusiasm, using almost the same "it's very fine—but, of course, there are a few points …" language that had rankled Robertson in earlier correspondence.

Davies lifted his drink and emptied it in one swallow. He set the glass down slowly with exaggerated delicacy, folded his hands together on top of the manuscript, and leaned in toward Maclean. In a voice the volume of a whisper but with the articulation of a courtroom prosecutor, he asked, "What are all these changes you want me to make? Should I change my men to women? Do you want me to put the beginning at the end?"

The ensuing conversation went round and round for almost an hour, with more drinks. Conclusion: a definitive agreement to publish.

In a tone that sounded markedly like an intended wrapping up of the meeting, Maclean said, "Yes, well, I'm sure we can work out the other details in the editing, but I must say, Robertson, that the title, *Fifth Business*, does leave me baffled. Would you be amenable to including an explanation at the beginning of the book?"

Davies winked at Derry, reached into his jacket pocket, and with a dramatic flourish, yanked out a scrap of paper. He unravelled it, laid it on top of his manuscript, and gracefully flattened out the wrinkled edges. He passed it to Maclean, who read it slowly, smiled, and passed it on around the table. Written in Davies's beautiful italic handwriting, it read as follows:

"Fifth Business"—definition

Those roles which, being neither those of Hero nor Heroine, Confidante nor Villain, but which were nonetheless essential to bring about the Recognition or dénouement, were called the Fifth Business in drama and opera companies organized according to the old style; the player who acted these parts was often referred to as Fifth Business.
—Tho. Overskou, Den Danske Skueplads

"Very good," Maclean said. "That'll do nicely. I think we're done here."

Davies nodded.

"By the way, can you tell me about the source of the quote?" Maclean asked.

"Oh, it's an obscure account of 19th-century theatre in Denmark that I came across many years ago. I can't remember when or where I found it, but I was intrigued by the concept and made a note of it and of the reference. I thought it might come in handy someday. And voilà."

"Fine," said Maclean. "I'd suggest we include this quote on the page before the table of contents or on the reverse side of the contents page. Agreed?"

They all lifted their glasses and said in unison, "Agreed."

Nice sleight of hand, Davies thought to himself. *Before anyone discovers that I've totally fabricated the reference source,* Fifth Business *will be published, translated into many languages, and considered a classic by enraptured readers around the world.*

He was right.

———————

As he walked off the stage at the Stratford Festival's Avon Theatre, Davies hesitated and listened to the continuing applause. The Sunday morning lecture had gone well. The near-capacity audience had been warm and enthusiastic. He turned around to look again at the lectern at centre stage, standing now abandoned amidst the props for Elliot Hayes's adaptation of his novel *World of Wonders,* the third in the Deptford Trilogy, of which *Fifth Business* had been the first.

The festival's inclusion in their 1992 season of a play based on one of his novels was a particular source of pride for him. It was still early in the season, and already *World of Wonders* was garnering critical and public acclaim.

Davies breathed in deeply, savouring the theatrical and literary success of the moment. It helped to salve wounds that had festered from earlier productions of his plays that—not to put too fine a point on it—had been poorly received by press and public. Urjo Kareda in the *Toronto Star* called a St. Lawrence Centre production of his play *Question Time* "a very grand, ambitious, and idiosyncratic disaster," and his play *Love and Libel* had bombed on Broadway. Clive Barnes in the *New York Times* savaged the production. A shudder rippled through Davies's core as he remembered the review.

His Stratford Festival connection went back a long time—a member of the first Board of Governors after the festival's founding in 1952; many guest lectures over the years; attendance at innumerable performances. So many fine friends he had from his years of association here. He was looking forward to dinner tonight at the Stratford home of writer Timothy Findlay and his partner, Bill Whitehead. Davies thought back to an evening when he had hosted the two of them recently at the Massey College High Table, and Tiff had asked him about Thornton Wilder, whom Davies had known. With a touch of uncharacteristic self-admonishment, Davies resolved to apologize tonight to Tiff for having dismissed the question with something to the effect of, "Wilder? Humph. Repressed homosexual." He knew that many people mistook his establishment demeanour for conservatism. He must remember to tell Tiff how he had written Jamie Cunningham, "I applaud you for your courage to be yourself," and how he had commended Douglas LePan after the publication of his book of homoerotic poetry, saying, "Douglas, this is very brave of you—not that I have ever given much attention to that side of my character."

His train of thought was interrupted by the prodding of his Stratford Festival handlers, who were encouraging Davies to make his way from backstage to the book-signing table in the lobby. The line of fans was long, perhaps numbering two hundred people, each clutching new or well-worn copies of his books, anxious for them to be signed—something to show off to grandchildren.

There were in fact two tables and two lines. Davies glanced at the one on which the Festival Store had piles of his various titles, doing a brisk business in sales. He smiled and mumbled under his breath, "Ka-ching, ka-ching, ka-ching," but then he immediately scowled and grumbled sotto voce, "Why the hell do these supposedly literate people not already have copies of all my books?"

"Pardon me?" Pat Quigley. The festival's Director of Education turned around as they reached the signing table, and asked, "Is there something wrong, Robertson?" She paused with her hand resting on the back of the chair she was about to pull out for him.

"Nothing at all, Pat," he replied, his facial muscles reconfiguring themselves into a jovial expression. "Here, let me." He took a step sideways, pulled out the second chair, and gallantly invited her to sit. Pat, knowing well enough when not to pursue a question with Davies, nodded and slipped into the chair. He dropped down onto his chair and, still with the same too-broad smile, glanced up and addressed the first person in line. "Everything's just hunky-dory, isn't it, my dear?"

"Ah, ah ..." the woman stuttered.

"I said, everything's just hunky-dory. Don't you agree, madam?"

"Ah ... yes ... I guess so."

"You guess so? What, you don't think you got your money's worth from my lecture?"

Pat reached over and gently laid her hand on Davies's arm.

Still fixing the woman with the mixed-message expression but pivoting 90 degrees in tone—well, at least 45—Davies said, "Yes, I'm sure you did. Now, I see you've brought a few of my books for me to sign." He reached his hands up and took them from her.

"Oh, yes, please, Mr. Davies ... er ... Professor Davies, I mean. And your lecture was wonderful. Wonderful. I've read all of your books. I'm such a big fan ... and I made all my children read them ... or at least made them read more of your books than the ones that they were required to study in school ... and now I'm making sure that my grandchildren read a few of them too. Your writing is such an important part of our literary history in this country ... and it's a scandal that your books are not required reading as much as they used to be."

He finished signing the books and handed them back, not looking at the woman. He turned his head toward Pat and raised his eyebrows almost to the point of intersecting with his glistening white mane. She placed her hand again on his forearm and this time gave him an affectionate squeeze.

The signing continued with far too much chatting for Davies's taste. Pat looked on anxiously. The line was shortening too slowly. She had been getting signals from the staff. They needed to prepare the house for the afternoon matinee. She leaned over and whispered in Davies's ear. He listened with his eyes closed. Without looking up, he stretched out his arm, ready to receive the next person's book. Nothing was placed in his hand. He wiggled his fingers: gimme, gimme. Still nothing.

Davies opened his eyes and jerked his head up, glaring impatiently at the next in line. A young man stood rigidly clasping a copy of *Fifth Business* with both hands against his breast. A tweed jacket with leather elbow patches hung loosely over his gawky frame. A stained tie was knotted tightly at the fraying collar of his white shirt.

"You would like Professor Davies to sign it?" Pat Quigley interjected encouragingly.

"Yes, please." With both hands, the young man lowered his copy and deposited it on the table, letting his fingers linger on it for a moment before straightening up and dropping his arms to his sides. "This, sir … is my favourite copy … of the various editions that I have. It's the public library copy that I read … the first time I read *Fifth Business*." Almost under his breath, he added, "When I was 8."

Davies looked up at him. "Eight?"

"Yes … sir."

Davies ran his fingers over the cover for a moment and then opened the book to the title page. He squinted and lifted the book closer to examine a faded red stamp:

TORONTO
PUBLIC
LIBRARIES

— — —

Travelling branch

SINCE THIS BOOK IS
NO LONGER IN DEMAND,
TORONTO PUBLIC LIBRARY
IS OFFERING IT FOR SALE

Davies raised his head and looked at the young man, whose lip was quivering slightly. Davies shook his head, picked up his pen, and wrote the following beside the stamp:

> *Rejected!—and by a public library! Can ignominy go further? It is as though Helen of Troy were rejected by a high school teachers' union!*

He closed the book and handed it to the young man. Screwing the cap back on his pen and placing it into the breast pocket of his jacket, he pushed his chair back and stood up.

"Ah, Robertson?" Pat Quigley stood up as well.

"Sorry, Pat, I have an important engagement," Davies replied. Then, looking out over the crowd, he bellowed, "Ladies and gentlemen, the signing session is now over."

He walked out from behind the table and put his arm around the young man's shoulders. "You and I, my boy, are going to lunch. So, you read it when you were 8 years old, you say. What was it about the novel ..."

References

Davies, Robertson. *At My Heart's Core*. Toronto: Clarke, Irwin, & Company, 1950.

Davies, Robertson. *Fifth Business*. Toronto: The Macmillan Company of Canada, 1970.

Grant, Judith Skelton. *Robertson Davies—Man of Myth: A Biography*. Toronto: Penguin Books Canada, 1994.

Ross, Val. *Robertson Davies—A Portrait in Mosaic*. Toronto: McClelland & Stewart, 2008.

faggots and faith

PATRICK IS LISTENING, SORT OF, TO THE PRE-
opera talk. It's Francis Poulenc's *Dialogue of the Carmelites* this
evening.

He leans against the banister and scans the crowd in the lobby.
Mainly older. Mainly white. Mainly straight. He steps back and
props himself against the wall, cupping his hands around his
phone screen as he swipes his finger down Grindr's home page.

There must be some cultured, attractive, eligible gay men here,
he hopes. Grindr tells him that there aren't any users online closer
than five hundred feet. So no cute gay men here tonight, at least
not yet, at least not on Grindr.

It's been four years since Evan died. Damn pancreatic cancer.

Patrick and Evan had been opera subscribers for decades,
and over the years they'd been to countless performances in other
cities around the world—Covent Garden, La Scala, La Fenice,
Palais Garnier, Opéra Bastille, Bolshoi, Vienna, Sydney. They'd
never gotten to Bayreuth. It had been on their list. They'd run
out of time.

Patrick's attention pivots back to the speaker when he hears
mention about tension between Poulenc's homosexuality and his
fervid Catholic faith. It's only a passing reference. By the time
it has registered in Patrick's brain, the speaker has moved on to
aspects of tonight's production.

Patrick is taken aback. *How did I not know that about Poulenc?*

We saw a production of Carmelites *in the mid-1980s … guess we didn't know enough about Poulenc's life then … or maybe Evan did know and didn't mention it … too close to home.*

Patrick pulls his right hand away from his phone screen and rests his arms against the wall behind to steady himself.

He resolves to learn more about Poulenc.

———

Francis Poulenc's music reflected his life, starting out light and airy in his early career in 1920s Paris while he was living an essentially faux heterosexual life and while he was nominally a Roman Catholic. But then his composing became emotional, conflicted, and profound when he began to live more openly as a gay man in 1929, and even more so after his dramatic conversion in 1936 to a theologically doctrinaire Catholicism.

That is something of an oversimplification, but not by much. Poulenc himself acknowledged, "What is most paradoxical in my work: the juxtaposition of the profane and the secular."

Expressing his homosexuality openly and yet immersing himself in a Catholic faith that condemned such a lifestyle seem to have battled against one another in his artistic imagination during the latter half of his career, leading to a variety of master works of searing intensity, including *Dialogue of the Carmelites*.

———

Evan's face was ashen, yet his eyes flashed terror and rage, as he crashed into their apartment after work that day in mid-September 1976.

This was not the same man who had ambled out the door that morning simultaneously whistling and humming while heading off to the second week with his new class of 11-year-old students. It was Evan's fifth year of teaching. The school board administrators wanted him to move to a secondary school where they felt his strong masculine presence would be more valuable. But he preferred working with children of primary school age. Evan wanted to concentrate on children in their early formative years.

"What's ... what's the matter?" Patrick asked, shaken by this volcanic entrance. After only a month being together, they were still feeling their way with each other.

"I need a drink. Now." Evan dropped his briefcase on the floor, threw his gym bag on top of it, and collapsed down onto the sofa. Without taking his shoes off, he stretched out full length, his head cradled in the pillows at one end and his legs kicking up against the other. Patrick headed into the kitchen to pour Evan's rye and ginger, and a vodka on the rocks for himself.

Placing the glass quietly on the coffee table within Evan's reach, Patrick leaned over and lightly kissed Evan's arm that lay across his closed eyes. He didn't react. Patrick stepped back, sat down in the chair opposite, and waited.

After a few moments, Evan said, "Johnson was parked outside the apartment when I left this morning. Waiting for me."

"Who?"

"Jesus Christ, Patrick," he hollered. "Johnson, my fucking principal." Patrick almost spilled his drink. This was the first time Evan had ever raised his voice to his new lover. Or swore. He didn't approve of swearing, including Patrick's. "Never take the name of the Lord in vain," Evan would chastise Patrick, gently but with conviction. It was an element of Evan's rigorous Catholic commitment. Not swearing had been part of Patrick's liberal Protestant upbringing as well, but he was more lax about adherence.

"Oh, yes," Patrick said. "What the ... what was he doing here?"

Jerking his head up off the pillow, Evan grabbed at his tie already loosened around his collar, struggled for a few moments with the knot, gave up, and yanked it up over his head. He crumpled the tie into a ball and, with the pitcher's form Patrick had witnessed on the mound during the late summer games, fastballed it toward the piano. A silk tie, not having the heft of a hard ball, it dropped well short of the target, ending up bedraggled across the far end of the sofa. Evan glared at it and shouted, "Wimp."

He dropped his head back down onto the pillow. Bringing both arms up, he pressed the balls of his palms into his eye sockets.

Patrick waited. This was such foreign territory.

Eventually, Evan let his arms slide down beside his body. His eyes opened and he stared up at the ceiling. "He wanted to know what I was doing here, leaving for school from this apartment building. He asked why I wasn't at my house up by the school."

Patrick waited.

Evan just lay there, staring at the ceiling, saying nothing, ignoring his drink.

"Well … what does it matter to him?" Patrick asked. "And how did he know you were here?"

Evan turned his head and looked at Patrick. His eyes were wet. "He says … he says that the school board has received information … a tip"—his chest was heaving as he made short intakes of breath, his eyes riveted on Patrick's—"rumours … that I'm living with a man."

———— ～ ————

The pre-performance lecture is over. Patrick moves into the hall and takes his regular seat on the aisle. There's always someone different in what had been Evan's seat beside him. Patrick politely nods good evening.

Through a contact in the membership office, Evan had arranged for their subscription seats to be in the front row. It makes reading the surtitles difficult, not that they were all that interested in doing so. They liked being able to see their friends

Sylvia and Jerome playing in the orchestra pit. It was also nice not to have bobbing heads in front obstructing their view of the stage.

Patrick's mind wanders off. In the early 1990s while singing in the gay men's chorus, he had travelled with the choir to a festival of gay choruses held that year in Seattle. One of the choruses, maybe the one from Chicago, performed the dramatic final scene of *Dialogue of the Carmelites*, in which the Carmelite nuns, one by one, are guillotined by the French revolutionary state for upholding their faith. In the performance in Seattle, members of the choir left the stage one at a time to the sound of a jarring crash that was to represent the guillotine. In those days of the 1990s, when so many of their friends were dying of AIDS, the impact of the performance was riveting.

The lights are dimmed. The curtain is raised. There is no prelude, immediately getting into the story and the emotion of fear scored by Poulenc to reflect the nervousness of Blanche about the rioting French citizens and the mounting Reign of Terror. Blanche pleads with her father to let her go live in a convent.

Patrick realizes that he's gripping the seat armrests. He wills himself to relax.

On July 17, 1794, a French Revolutionary tribunal sentenced to death sixteen sisters of the Roman Catholic Carmelite religious order from Compiègne northeast of Paris for engaging in counterrevolutionary activities. The nuns had continued to observe liturgical practices of prayer and worship that had been banned by the newly installed civil authorities. The French Revolutionaries had targeted the Catholic Church, along with the monarchy and the aristocracy, as the key actors responsible for oppression of the French people.

Later that day, the 16 women were guillotined in Paris.

A 17th member in the Order, Sister Marie de l'Incarnation,

escaped the fate of her sisters and wrote a record of the martyrdom of the Carmelite nuns.

In 1931, German novelist Gertrude von Le Fort published a novella, *Die Letzte am Schafott*, based on this account of the Carmelites' martyrdom that she had discovered in the archives of the Munich University Library. Le Fort was disturbed by the rise of the Nazis in Germany at the time and by the general unwillingness of the public, including people of faith, to object and resist. She saw in the story of the Carmelites an inspirational tale of courage, conviction, and commitment to the spiritual principles of the Catholic faith.

Two decades later, Le Fort's novella inspired a play by French author George Bernanos entitled *Dialogue des Carmélites*, which in turn served as the basis for Poulenc's opera. Though the basic storyline remained essentially the same, the underlying themes and emotional thrusts evolved over the three works, reflecting the respective preoccupations of Le Fort, Bernanos, and Poulenc.

In Poulenc's hands, the music and the lyrics evoke deep psychological and spiritual conflicts. The opera is not one of action as much as one of monologues and dialogues through which Poulenc grapples with the complicated juxtaposing of fear and courage, of living by and dying for one's principles, of commitment to and antipathy against a Catholicism that leads, seemingly inexorably, to sacrifice, martyrdom, and death.

"He kept scowling at me across the table and mouthing 'faggot,'" Evan said quietly, deadpanning.

They were sitting on the sofa side by side, Patrick's arm wrapped around Evan, Evan's head leaning on Patrick's shoulder. Spread out on the coffee table in front of them were pages of yellow foolscap with notes that they had been making for debriefing from today's session and preparing for the next one—strategies and counterstrategies, arguments and counterarguments.

In quiet, measured tones, Evan had been going over the day's negotiations—Evan and his lawyer on one side of the table in the Catholic School Board office arrayed against his principal, three School Board officials, and one of the Board's lawyers.

"My God," Patrick said. "What an asshole he is."

"And he is so conniving. Does it surreptitiously in ways so that the others can't see him. The Board lawyer almost caught him once or twice."

Evan stared down at their clasped hands. "He, my 'asshole' principal, as you so delicately describe him"—a flicker of a smile slipped across his lips, the first of its kind that evening—"knows he can't accuse me outright because they don't have any documented proof. They'd leave themselves open to libel charges. My lawyer keeps drilling me not to let anything slip that they could grab as proof."

Evan lifted his head off Patrick's shoulder and looked him in the eye. "That's what's killing me as much as anything," he said. "Having to lie. Not being able to shout at them all, 'Of course, I'm gay. And in love with a man and living in sin with him.' But that would be the end of it. They'd justify firing me on the basis of 'moral turpitude,' their catchy phrase for contravening the Church's teachings on homosexuality."

He flopped his head back on Patrick's shoulder. They sat quietly.

"What do you do when he says … mouths … 'faggot'?"

"I had been glaring back at him. But …" Evan took a few deep breaths. "Now, I just look away or close my eyes." He squeezed Patrick's hand harder. "It's been two months of these sessions. I'm so bloody tired."

"I know you are, Darling. Why don't you call in sick tomorrow? Take a rest day. You're so exhausted by all this stress and keeping up your full teaching schedule at the same time. It's too much."

Evan jerked his body upright. "No, no, no, no, no. They'd find some way to twist that around. They'd say that I'm not fulfilling my responsibilities, that I'm … what's the word? Malingering.

They'd try to use that to force me out. And tomorrow's Friday. I'll be taking my class to Mass. I wouldn't miss that. Ever."

———— ⌣ ————

During the intermission, Patrick heads up to the third-floor lobby to find a quiet corner and be alone. He's still reeling from the riveting portrayal of the Mother Superior in her deathbed scene. He's sat by too many bedsides, with too many agonizing dyings over the past few years—his mom's, his dad's, Evan's mom's, his brother's, Evan's.

"Patrick!"

Patrick, staring out the window and looking onto the street below, watches Gordie's and Frank's reflections as they make their way through the crowd. He likes them, but Gordie can be tiresome. Such a critical opera queen. Patrick turns around to face them as they reach him.

"Hi, guys," he says and extends his hand. Frank shakes his hand and furrows his brow as he looks into Patrick's eyes. Gordie throws his arms around Patrick and gives him a big bear hug. Patrick imagines droplets of Gordie's wine spilling out of his glass and down the back of the new shirt he had worn that night, intending to look his best on the off chance he might meet someone new and interesting and with potential.

"I must say," Gordie starts, "I'm not a fan of this ascetic approach in the set and lighting design. It's French Revolutionary times for heaven's sake. Shouldn't we have more decadent, Versailles-inspired décor? And what was with the thrashing around on the bed like that? She's dying, for heaven's sake. Make it a little more dignified."

"Gordie," Frank mumbles as he puts his arm around his partner's waist. Patrick smiles, knowing that the gesture that Frank always uses never works.

"And all the Catholic breast-beating and piety and guilt and sanctimoniousness. Almost makes me wish they could bump up the final scene, send them all to the guillotine right away, and then send all of us home, spared of two more acts of nauseating religiosity. Give me Giovanni's lustiness or Carmen's sexiness or Violetta's consumption or Cio-Cio San's dagger ... anything but more of this namby-pamby, maudlin, does-God-still-love me? what-does-God-want-me-to-do? dying-for-my-sins-or-your-sins-or-whoever's-sins crap. Honestly, why did they program *Carmelites*? Why does anyone program *Carmelites*? Poulenc should have stuck to orchestral or vocal work that I would never have had to be subjected to in an opera house. Oh jeez, Frank, would you hold my drink? I've got to hit the toilet. Actually, you can finish it. I'll see you back at our seats." Pecking Patrick on each cheek, he says, "Lovely to see you, Dear, as always," and rushes toward the washroom.

Frank and Patrick look at each other and take a deep breath.

"Sorry," Frank says. "He's a bit wound up tonight."

"Tonight?" Patrick chuckles.

Frank smiles. "You okay?" he asks.

Patrick hesitates and then shrugs.

"An evening like this must be difficult for you. I get it," Frank says. "That's probably presumptuous of me to say." He takes Patrick's hand and gives it a firm squeeze. "Buck up, boy. You're not alone."

"I know, thanks," Patrick replies as Frank walks away. *But I am.*

———

Francis Poulenc's early success as a composer and performer while still in his twenties opened social and artistic doors. He frequented the most vibrant Parisian salons, where he met and became friends with the likes of Picasso, Stravinsky, Colette, Britten, and Bernstein. While he was still in the throes of discovering his own sexual preferences, the diversity of his social network suited him well.

Poulenc was a regular at Le Boeuf sur la Toit, the gay demimonde's nightly gathering place. Opened in the early 1920s, Le Boeuf was the "crossroad of destinies, the cradle of loves, the matrix of disputes, the navel of Paris"—and the "navel of the navel, so to speak, was inevitably Cocteau." The eccentric and flamboyant gay writer Jean Cocteau was a good friend of Poulenc's. The two collaborated over the years on a number of artistic projects, with Poulenc putting to music some of Cocteau's poems and one play.

In 1928, Poulenc made an awkward proposal for a marriage of convenience to his childhood sweetheart, Raymonde Linnoisier. She turned him down, perhaps because of what she suspected to be his repressed homosexuality. In correspondence, she made clear her distaste for the "chic, idle, homosexual element" of those who had gathered for the funeral of composer Erik Satie. Poulenc was so distraught by Raymonde's rejection that he found himself unable to continue with a prestigious commission of a ballet, *Aubade*, to be choreographed by Nijinsky. He wrote to the patron who had commissioned it asking to be relieved of the assignment, since, "Life has broken me to such a point that I no longer know who I am." But then he fell in love.

Raymonde Linnoisier's rejection opened the path for the first truly passionate sexual and emotional relationship of his life, this time with a man. In 1929, he fell in love with painter and gallery owner Richard Chanlaire and found himself expressing fervour far more intense than the formal antiseptic love he had maintained over the years for Raymonde. He told Chanlaire, "You have changed my life, you are the sun of my thirty years, a reason for living and working ... my beloved friend, I huddle in your arms, my head against your heart."

To a close friend, Poulenc confided the pain of having to conceal his "great, grave secret," referring to his homosexuality as his "anomaly." He returned to work on *Aubade*, and the performance was held on schedule. With *Aubade* being based on the Roman myth of the goddess Diane, Poulenc has her railing against the divine law that has condemned her to perpetual virginity. Unable to escape her fate, she seeks an outlet for her sexual frustration by taking up a bow and launching herself into the forest to hunt for stags. The work vacillates between melancholy and mania. Poulenc was at the piano playing his music to accompany Nijinsky's choreography. The distraught anguish of the work and of its composer was palpable and at odds with the atmosphere of the party at which it was being premiered. Poulenc's ballet, the product of an artistic soul conflicted between personal passions and a public persona, received mixed reactions.

Evan snuggled deeper into Patrick's chest. Patrick manipulated the comforter with his feet and juggled it up close enough so that he could grab a hold of it. He pulled it up over their naked bodies. They were both still sweating from the sex, but the February cold in their apartment bedroom would soon overwhelm that.

Patrick leaned over and rested his lips on the top of Evan's head.

Evan let out a sigh and said, "God, so much of my life. What a waste of time."

Patrick didn't press him.

"Thirty years of pretending. Playing the perfect Catholic son. Playing the altar boy, the deacon, the youngest ever chair of Parish Council. Playing the superstar Catholic teacher. Playing the courting-good-Catholic-girls role. Playing the straight boy ... the straight man."

Patrick wrapped his arms around Evan tighter.

"I'd catch myself checking out a hot guy ... and then, wham, the Catholic guilt would come crashing in and I'd completely shut down that part of me."

Patrick leaned over and whacked Evan's bum. "Bad boy, naughty thoughts. Five Hail Marys."

Evan grabbed hold of Patrick's wrist and squeezed it hard. "Not funny, Babe."

Patrick pulled back.

"Then I finally accept who I really am, slut around for a couple of years with countless guys I'd never take home to Mother, and eventually meet a really decent man who"—he turned his head up toward Patrick's, closed the distance, and kissed him, keeping his eyes wide open this time—"is quickly evolving into the love of my life, And I think I am actually now getting all my shit together, but then suddenly I find myself on the verge of being kicked out of the one and only job that I've always wanted, refused the Eucharist by my priest … if Father Clarence even still is my priest … told not to step into my parents' house until I 'dispense with all this foolishness' …"

Despite his best intentions, Patrick was on the verge of dozing off. It had been a long day. Evan suddenly jumped out of bed and started pacing around the room. "How am I going to pay my share of the rent if this last appeal goes against me? Shit." He grabbed the footboard and jerked it up and down, letting it crash each time onto the floor. Patrick was wide awake.

"Evan. The neighbours downstairs."

"Fuck the bloody neighbours … fuck the bloody school board … fuck the bloody Catholic Church … fuck my bloody parents …"

Patrick watched as Evan stood gripping the footboard, his arm muscles taut, his eyes shut, his lips quivering.

Quietly, Patrick said, "Evan … Evan." Evan slowly relaxed, opened his eyes, and looked back at Patrick. Patrick smiled and said, "Evan … come back to bed and … fuck me."

Patrick is usually quick out of his seat and heading to the exit as the final curtain comes down. Get to the subway before the crowds. He's not one for ritualistic standing ovations. He'll join in only if the production and performances merit it. Tonight, they do. But he is not on his feet.

He sits. A few patrons squeeze past him and he shifts his knees to let them by. On stage, the cast is taking their bows, smiling at the rapturous applause that's filling the house. In the pit, the orchestra members are packing up their instruments and chatting enthusiastically with each other. It's been a good night. Everyone is pleased.

Sylvia comes over to the edge of the pit and stands looking up at Patrick. Jerome joins her, and taps on the railing to get Patrick's attention. Patrick flinches, gives them two thumbs up, perches over the rail to shake their hands, and then slumps back in his seat again. Sylvia and Jerome smile and turn and leave.

The hall is emptying. Patrick is the only one left in his row. Opera without Evan is still opera. And it's not. Tonight, after the ambush during the lecture, and now with the intensity of this performance, it's even more so. Of both.

Yet, that alone doesn't explain it. Sure, Poulenc's music for the *Salve Regina* as Blanche joins the other sisters stepping slowly but resolutely toward their deaths is powerful, gorgeous, heart-rending. But Patrick, still not able to breathe, is immobilized by the sisters' willingness to accept that fate.

He shakes himself, forcibly relaxing his diaphragm, taking a deep breath, holding it, letting it out. "For God's sake, it's just an opera … a 200-year-old story," he mumbles. But it's not. For Patrick, it's not just an opera. It's not just a centuries-old story. It's right here and now, in this empty seat beside him.

———

Poulenc's conversion in 1936 from a nominal to a deeply committed Roman Catholic was mystical and radical. But his case was hardly an isolated one. For almost fifty years from the mid-1880s onward, many writers, artists, and intellectuals embraced Roman Catholicism with fervour.

The Catholic Church had felt under siege in France ever since the time of the Revolution. But this intensified in a "reactionary revolution" after the country's crushing military defeat by Prussia in 1870–71 and the social chaos that accompanied the rise and subsequent repression of the socialist Paris Commune of 1871.

That the church, as an institution, would organize to reassert its power is not a surprise. It is perplexing that the intellectual and artistic elite, both heterosexuals and homosexuals, not only joined in this conservative movement but also, in essence, became its militant vanguard. Their commitment seems to have been far greater than the devotion of the ordinary Catholic of the time. That contrast intensified their resolve. They came to believe that, since the populace at large had become seduced by modernity's secularism, it was their responsibility as intellectual and artistic leaders to redeem the country.

Why were so many prominent homosexual writers, artists, and intellectuals amongst the reactionary revolution's most ardent champions, including in the later period between WWI and WWII, the time of Poulenc's conversion? Why were they such advocates for Catholicism when the church to which they were pledging their allegiance and to which they were committing artistic energies was vociferously hostile to their sexual orientation and virulently denouncing the sexual acts to which they were committing their bodies?

The poet, writer, and playwright Jean Cocteau was the most high-profile homosexual member of this coterie. Cocteau was shattered by the death of his lover Raymond Radiguet at the young age of 20 in a Parisian clinic on December 12, 1923. Friends introduced Cocteau to two disparate conduits to assuage his grief—opium and religious conversion. And with the theatricality for which he was already famous, Cocteau embraced both simultaneously. When challenged by the proponents of the

Catholic Orthodoxy to relinquish his multiple sinful ways, Cocteau initially resisted but eventually agreed to enter a detoxification clinic (into which he smuggled a new young male lover). Upon release, he resumed active indulgence in both addictions—opium and young men.

But Cocteau didn't abandon the Catholicism that was pressuring him to renounce his passions, particularly his sexual lifestyle, which was the one more explicitly censured in dogma. Jacques Maritain, one of the leaders in the conservative Catholic movement, admonished Cocteau, explaining that homosexual love in the eyes of the Church violates both divine and natural law, "a profound refusal of the Cross." Cocteau responded that he "needed love and to make love to souls," implying without subtlety that he relished those souls being present in beautiful male bodies. In 1928, Cocteau published the highly autobiographical *Le Livre Blanc*, in which he affirmed both his homosexuality and his faith.

The circumstances leading up to Poulenc's conversion to fervid Catholicism in August 1936 had parallels to those in Cocteau's situation. Poulenc had been shaken by the deaths of a number of close friends and professional colleagues. His finances had suffered with the collapse of the Lyon-Allemand bank. He was unnerved by political and social upheaval in France and by the outbreak of the civil war in Spain on July 18, 1936, which was followed shortly afterwards by the assassination of gay poet Frederico García Lorca. A few years later, Poulenc dedicated his 1943 Violin Concerto to Lorca's memory.

These traumas exacerbated the melancholy and frustration that had characterized much of his adult life.

Though Poulenc was experiencing some degree of romantic stability, having begun a relationship with Raymond Destouches, a taxi driver he had met in the early 1930s, professionally his composing had begun to shift from the light and airy works of his earlier career to more contemplative approaches as reflected in the Concerto for Organ, String Orchestra, and Timpani that he described as grave and austere.

On August 22, 1936, having been stunned by news of the decapitation in a car accident in Hungary of fellow French composer Pierre-Octave Ferroud, Poulenc made a pilgrimage with a few friends to Notre-Dame de Rocamadour. As a site of charismatic intensity, the Black Virgin of Rocamadour carries a weight almost comparable to the better-known Black Virgin of Montserrat near Barcelona. The religious site is set dramatically into a cliff face overlooking the gorge of the river Alzor in southern France. Inside, a black statue of the Virgin Mary is mounted in a tiny crypt-like chapel carved out of the rock reached by a stone staircase of 223 steps. Something happened to Poulenc on that day in his encounter with the Black Virgin of Rocamadour— some sort of riveting conversion to a deeper faith that crystallized the momentum in his composing to a much more profound and spiritual intensity.

The focus around which that intensity revolved was suffering— suffering as the explicit theme of much of his subsequent work, and suffering as the essential precondition for his most significant artistic creativity.

The envelope lay unopened on the table between them. It was of the vellum-matted variety, with the embossed logo, name, and address of the Catholic School Board in the upper left corner, definitely not the type used for mass mailings. Evan's name was neatly typed in rich black ink—a "Mr." before and a comma and "Esq." following. The address used was Patrick's apartment, not Evan's house.

"I never gave them this address. It's on none of my files. How fucking presumptuous of them to use it in order to send this here."

"Galling."

"Vindictive."

Patrick laid his hand on top of Evan's to quench Evan's nervous tapping. "They've done their research. You gotta grant them that," Patrick said.

"Word has it they keep a few PIs on retainer. We've probably been followed, maybe for months. How creepy."

Patrick got up and walked around the kitchen. He picked the coffee canister up off the counter and, putting one hand on the lid, turned it upside down to examine the bottom. He grabbed the ceramic teddy bear cookie jar, a purchase from their outing the previous Saturday to the flea market, lifted the top off, and looked inside.

"What are you doing?" Evan said.

"Checking for hidden cameras, microphone bugs."

Despite himself, Evan chuckled. "Ha-ha-ha."

Patrick came back to the table and took a hold of the neck of his chair. Balancing the chair on one leg, he swivelled it around until the back faced the table. He sat down straddling the seat, crossed his arms on the neck of the chair, and rested his chin on his forearms, staring at the envelope. "Well, are you going to open it?"

Evan crept his fingers across the Arborite surface to within a few inches of the envelope, hesitated, and then pulled his hand back. "Clearly if I open it, that'll be proof that I received it, here at your place."

"Clearly, my dear, they know you're here."

"Fuck."

Evan looked over at Patrick. "I'm so sorry, my dear. You didn't sign up for this."

"You don't know what it says."

Evan took a deep breath and said, "Yes, I do. We both do. This is the end of the line."

Patrick squeezed Evan's hand. "We'll figure something out. We can live on one salary for a while."

Evan shook his head and looked down at the envelope. "What am I going to tell my kids? They'll think I've abandoned them."

"My guess is," Patrick said, hesitating, "that you won't have a chance. Johnson won't let you back in the school."

"Jesus Christ!"

Evan pulled his hand out of Patrick's, clenched his fist, and pounded the table. The envelope jumped off the table surface and skidded toward the edge, stopping just shy of falling off. Patrick whacked the table and the envelope slipped a bit further. Evan took a turn, and then Patrick again.

Patrick said, "Together. On three." They both raised their fists above their heads. "One … two … three." Crash.

They left the envelope on the floor where it had fallen and went to bed.

Patrick fumbles with his keys at the door. He had walked home from the opera, distracted, stepping out into the path of oncoming traffic more than once. He opens the door, drops his coat on the hall floor, and goes directly into the library. Opening the glass bookcase doors, he reaches up to the shelf of picture albums and pulls several of them out, laying them on the large oak table that serves as his desk, that had served as both of their desks.

What year was it? 1988? '89?

The first one he opens has photos of their early travels, celebration parties, and weekends at the cottage they bought in 1980. Too early. He closes it and opens the next one, and within the first few pages finds pictures of the Barcelona trip—Gaudí's Sagrada Família, their hotel on Las Ramblas, the Fundació Joan Miró. Patrick rests his hand on the plastic sleeve covering the prints and pauses for a moment. What he's looking for will be on the next page.

He turns the page. The photo is more striking than he had

remembered. Evan is leaning nonchalantly on a railing. He's beautiful—trim, muscular, a large moustache approaching handlebar size, a full head of dark brown hair with a matching tuft poking up above the top button of his pale yellow shirt. He is wearing black-frame sunglasses, a blue nylon windbreaker zipped halfway up, and khaki dress slacks. One hand is lodged into his pants pocket; the other hand, on the arm that's resting on the railing, bears a silver band on his fourth finger.

Patrick lifts his hand and kisses its twin on his fourth finger.

In the background behind Evan is the riveted serrated mountain face plummeting down three hundred metres to a complex of beige-coloured buildings perched on a ledge a thousand metres above the valley floor—the ancient Benedictine monastery of Santa Maria de Montserrat.

Evan appears relaxed and yet taut. His lips are parted ever so slightly. There is not a smile, more of a … what?

He had made his pilgrimage—he had prayed at the 12th-century Romanesque statue of the Black Virgin of Montserrat.

Visiting Montserrat was one of the main reasons Evan had wanted to go to Barcelona. And once they had arrived at the monastery, Evan had gone quiet. There were crowds, but Evan, usually so impatient at sites overrun with tourists, had been oblivious to them. That was one of the first clues for Patrick to keep his mouth shut. He just followed a few steps behind as Evan patiently made his way up to the statue's sanctuary at the rear of the chapel. Eventually, they were standing directly in front of the altar. Bright gold covered the robed bodies of the Madonna and the Christ child, accentuating their black faces. Jesus, perched on Mary's lap, initially looked grotesque to Patrick's skeptical eyes, hardly a baby, more like a miniature adult. But, he had had to admit to himself, their expressions were gentle, compassionate, welcoming.

Just then the organ reverberated through the church with the opening chords of the Virolai, the hymn to Our Lady of

Montserrat sung daily at noon by the 50-member boys' choir. Patrick listened to the angelic voices. He didn't get the reverence, but he could appreciate aesthetic beauty. "Rosa d'abril, Morena de la serra ..."

Oh my God, Patrick had thought. *Rosa d'abril ... April rose, dark-skinned lady of the mountain. Evan's birthday is in April.* Patrick watched as Evan's back started swaying, his shoulders dropping, his arms twitching. Patrick moved closer to support him. Evan's body steadied. He crossed himself. Patrick saw tears streaming down Evan's face.

<hr />

Francis Poulenc's musical compositions in the years after the spiritual experience at Rocamadour evoke an intense suffering soul—suffering from the tragedies in the world around him, from the loves and losses in his personal life, and from the conflict between the spiritual commitments of his heart and the Church's abhorrence of how he expressed his love with his body. Poulenc's powerful choral work, *Figure humaine,* based on the texts by his friend the poet Paul Éluard, elevated Poulenc's reputation to that of *the* musical voice of the French resistance movement against the Nazis. The death of his friend the gay artist and designer Christian Bérard at the young age of forty-seven in 1949 inspired Poulenc to write his *Sabat Mater* and dedicate it to Bérard's memory—just the most recent of a long list of intimate friendships cut short by tragic or violent deaths.

And then came *Dialogues des Carmélites* begun in 1953, the work that Poulenc believed, more than any other, was a reflection of the tortured and sacrificial life that he himself was living. He identified with the story and with the characters. Referring to himself as "un éternal inquiet," he saw in the conflicted Blanche an embodiment of his own struggles as his personal and professional self-doubts that verged at times on utter self-contempt battled against his profound spiritual aspirations.

Poulenc had met Lucien Roubert sometime in the late 1940s and had been consumed by his love for the younger man ever since. It was hardly an easy relationship. Poulenc's burgeoning musical career required him to travel much of the time, leaving Lucien stuck in his hometown of Toulon on the Mediterranean in southern France. Furthermore, Poulenc was still in love with his longtime driver, Raymond Destouches, and even though that relationship had evolved into a platonic one, Lucien was understandably jealous. There had been separations and reconciliations.

Then, in February 1955, just after returning from a triumphant performance of his Concerto for Two Pianos with Benjamin Britten in London's Royal Festival Hall, Poulenc learned that Lucien had been diagnosed with tuberculosis. At first, the case did not appear serious. Over the next months, Lucien seemed to recover. By August, a reversal had set in, and Poulenc moved his now critically ill lover into a clinic in Cannes. Staying in the nearby Hotel Majestic to be close to Lucien, Poulenc worked on the final scenes of the opera for several months before eventually retreating to his home in Noizay to write the music for the scaffold scene.

Francis Poulenc's hand could hardly keep up with the music taking shape in his head as he scribbled away at the piano in his chateau at Noizay. It was torturous, excruciating—not the mechanics of transcribing the melodies and orchestrations onto the page, but rather the searingly poignant beauty of what was flowing out of him. The climactic scene of his new opera *Dialogue des Carmélites* was nearing completion, with the young novice Blanche mounting the scaffold to join her religious sisters, guillotined for their faith.

At that same moment, Poulenc's lover Lucien lay dying in Cannes.

"I have finished," Poulenc said to his housekeeper as he laid his pen down on the manuscript paper. He meant the opera. But he knew too, in his soul, that the same applied to his lover's life.

"Monsieur Lucien will die now," he added quietly.

He was right.

———⌣———

Evan had dozed off, the painkillers the nurse provided finally taking effect. Patrick, sitting in the chair beside Evan's hospital bed, had read through the morning paper cover to cover. Twice. The reports of the X-ray and CAT scan seemed to be taking forever. The two of them had come to Emergency 12 hours earlier bearing the recent blood work results that had so alarmed Evan's GP.

A movement caught the corner of Patrick's eye. He looked toward the door. Dr. Levan was leaning against the doorjamb, a large black binder tucked under his arm, watching Evan curled fetal position in bed, the sheets half covering his body, half not. Their eyes met. Patrick wrinkled his brow. Levan shook his head.

"I am awake, you guys." Evan's eyes were closed, but the reedy small voice was his.

Dr. Levan stepped into the room, closed the door, and walked over to the end of the bed. In a quiet, measured tone, he said, "I'm sorry that it's taken so long to get the report. But ... there was so much to document."

Evan moved to tuck a pillow behind his back so that he could sit up straighter. Patrick jumped to help him. Once settled, Evan nodded to Patrick to sit beside him on the bed. Patrick did, gingerly avoiding leaning against Evan's abdomen, which had been the location of so much pain the past few months.

"I'm sorry, gentlemen. It's very bad news. Pancreatic cancer. Stage four. The pancreas is completely engulfed. Abrasions on the liver. Indications of growths in the lungs. And it has spread into the lymph nodes. I'm afraid with it progressed so extensively, so aggressively, there are no treatment options ... no realistic treatment options that we can offer."

There must have been more conversation. But most everything was a blur after that in Patrick's memory. He sort of remembered Dr. Levan talking about admitting Evan, and both he and Evan declining, as if they had discussed this in advance. They just both knew they wanted to be at home. In-home palliative care services could be arranged. Patrick does remember hearing that from Levan. But how they got Evan out of the emergency room bed and dressed, how they got downstairs to the car, how he drove home and got Evan back up to their condo and in their own bed—all a fog.

Now Patrick sat staring at his computer screen, struggling to compose an e-mail message to their close friends and family. The phone would have been useless at that point. He wouldn't have been able to talk. But he figured he could break the news to the others electronically.

Patrick was roused from his communion with the computer screen by totally out-of-context noises coming from the bedroom. Evan had awakened and was laughing, not a little giggle but hearty robust laughter. Patrick ran into the bedroom. Evan's eyes were radiant.

"My God, I don't believe it. You won't believe it. I've just been having the most unbelievable dream." More laughter. He was shaking.

Patrick leapt onto the bed and grabbed his arm. "Tell me. Tell me. What's happening? Are you okay?"

"Okay? I'm incredible. I've never felt so incredible."

Gasping for breath, he tried to put words to his exhilaration. "I've just been walking in the garden with Jesus. It was so wonderful. We were joking and kibitzing. Patrick, he told me that I looked so sexy. And my God, was He hot too."

Patrick didn't know whether to laugh or cry. He was just awestruck. How could he pivot from a day of shock to this? What was this? Was Evan for real?

Calming down a degree, Evan looked Patrick straight in the

eyes and said, "Don't worry—I haven't gone bonkers. This is really wonderful. Honestly, it's going to be okay. Jesus says that I have nothing to worry about or feel guilty about. I should drop any of the burdens I've been carrying. I'm loved. He loves me. He's ready for me. Everything is going to be okay. The pain will be over. I'm going soon."

Evan stopped and took a long, deep breath. He lay back quietly.

Patrick walks from his den, leaving the photo album open on his desk, and heads into the living room. He doesn't turn on any lights. The small night light over the stove is on. Beams from tonight's full moon, or nearly full moon, flood in through the picture windows. He takes a tumbler down from the shelf, lifts the Laphroaig bottle off the sideboard, and pours himself a generous portion. He crosses the room and drops down into his reading chair. He places the glass on the small table beside his chair. Glimmers of moonlight reflect off the amber surface of the Scotch. Shifting around slightly in his chair, he cranes his neck to look up at the moon. He squints.

Where is that face?

Evan could never understand why Patrick had such difficulty making out the man in the moon. It was a running jibe, one of many he directed at Patrick. No one teases Patrick like that anymore. All his friends treat him so differentially now. Patrick chalks it up to the widow business.

Failing yet again to figure out how the pattern of eyes, nose, and mouth are supposedly configured, Patrick drops his gaze back to earth and the city skyline. A column of moonlight lies placidly across the landscape, heading in Patrick's direction. Or so it seems. It's past midnight. The downtown offices are black hulks at this hour, with only a splattering of floors lit up for late-working staff or cleaners.

Patrick takes a sip of his drink, closes his eyes, and relishes the smoky peaty texture sliding down his throat. "Your ashtray Scotch," Evan used to call it. Another jibe. Patrick holds the tumbler with both hands and breathes in the aroma.

He looks over at the baby grand piano resting sedately in the alcove. Evan taught so many children and adults on that instrument over the years, having reinvented himself as a music teacher after being terminated by the school board. Patrick scolds himself for not being more disciplined in practicing. There's not the same motivation as when he had to learn the accompaniments for Evan's singing of Schubert's *Winterreise* and *Die Schoene Muellerin*, and those classical Italian songs and arias that Evan loved so much. Patrick cringes slightly remembering his floundering efforts even though Evan wasn't so critical. Patrick was better at playing the hymns for the quiet little devotions that Evan wanted each morning during those last weeks when he lay in the hospital bed that had been set up in their living room, right next to the piano— while he still had the lung capacity, while he could still sing a bit, speak a little. Patrick thinks it ironic that on the last of those occasions, the hymn Evan wanted was *Breathe on Me, Breath of God*. Or maybe it was not ironic. Not to Evan.

When Evan's father was dying, his mother made preparations with the funeral home and the cemetery. She bought a double niche to hold both his and eventually her ashes. Evan was horrified and asked, "What about the bodily resurrection?" His mother laughed. She couldn't believe that he still subscribed to traditional Catholic teaching opposing cremation. Evan had the good sense not to argue with his mother as she prepared for the imminent death of her husband. And over the years, Evan gradually reconciled himself to cremation both for his parents and for him and Patrick—reconciled, though never convincingly so. Begrudgingly. Evan grumbled but didn't object when Patrick bought the double niche next to his parents' for their own ashes.

Patrick's eyes trace the window ledge beside the piano and

fall onto the small white ceramic box. It had belonged to Evan's mother. She used to keep a bit of jewellery in it. She thought it pretty with the delicately painted designs. After she died, Evan brought it home. He thought it was more than pretty. The stylized fish on the lid gave it a sacred meaning—the early Christian symbol for Christ. His mother would have pooh-poohed that. Evan's mother and father had become less religious over the years, unlike Evan. His parents almost never went to Mass, certainly not like Evan did. Even after he was fired, he'd still go, as clandestinely as that had to be. He'd feel guilty for taking the Eucharist without having gone to confession first, which of course he couldn't or wouldn't do. And with no confession, there was no forgiveness for him either. At least that's what Evan said he felt on the few occasions when Patrick could get him to talk about it.

All that changed with the walk-in-the-garden-with-Jesus dream.

Patrick lifts himself up out of the chair and goes over to the piano. He runs his fingers lightly over the keyboard. He depresses the keys A-A-A-Bb-F-A and plays the three first bars of *Breathe on Me, Breath of God*. And then he repeats, more softly. He leans over and picks up the ceramic box from the window ledge and returns to his chair. Resting the box in his lap, Patrick traces the raised glazing of the fish symbol on the cover. He lifts the lid and stares at the tiny sealed bag of grey dust that he had taken out of the urn before the interment of Evan's ashes. Poking up ever so slightly from the midst of the ashes is a silver ring. Patrick lifts his right hand to his mouth and rests his lips on its twin on his finger.

References

Burton, Richard D. E. *Francis Poulenc*. London: Absolute Press, 2002.

Hallman, David G. *August Farewell—The Last Sixteen Days of a Thirty-Three-Year Romance*. Indianapolis: iUniverse, 2011.

Le Fort, Gertrud von. *The Song at the Scaffold*. Trans. from the 1931 original *Die Letzte am Schafott* by Olga Marx. San Francisco: Ignatius Press, 2011.

Poulenc, Francis. *Dialogue des Carmélites*. OEHMS Classics. ORF Radio-Symphonieorchester Wien under the direction of Bertrand de Billy. Recorded live January 2008 and April 2011.

Steegmuller, Francis. *Cocteau, a Biography*. Boston: Little, Brown, and Company, 1970.

Printed in the United States
By Bookmasters